Forgotten Royals

Alexis Jones

Published by Alexis Jones, 2024.

This is a work of fiction. Similarities to real people, places, or events are entirely coincidental.

FORGOTTEN ROYALS

First edition. October 21, 2024.

Copyright © 2024 Alexis Jones.

ISBN: 979-8227826022

Written by Alexis Jones.

Dedication

The Northshore Academy of Martial Arts Dojo crew. You were there when I was younger and I don't know if I would be at the place I'm at now. You guys have been my rock in the past and I love the dojo. Thank you for being there for me when I was younger and being there for me now.

Alexandru Jociva, Thank you for being a great sensei and always believing in me. If it weren't for you, I don't know if this would be possible. You have helped me through so much and continue to be there for me.

Matthew Hibbeler, Thank you for being there when I need you. We may have our ups and downs, but there is always something between us that is unbreakable. These past few years have been wonderful and I love being with you. Thank you for helping me with this book, and many more to come. There is always going to be us, and I appreciate everything you have done. I love you so much and I don't know where I would be without you.

Chapter 1: The Letter

Daniel sat on the edge of his bed, staring at the unassuming envelope that had arrived that morning. It was plain, yellowed with age, and sealed with a deep crimson wax that bore a symbol he didn't recognize. The faint scent of antiquity wafted from it, a whisper of secrets waiting to be uncovered. His heart raced as he picked it up, the weight of the letter heavy in his hands. He turned it over, running his fingers along the wax seal, half-expecting it to break apart at the slightest touch. But it remained intact, as if guarding the secrets contained within. Daniel's mind raced through possibilities. Was it junk mail? A misguided invitation? Or perhaps something more sinister? With a deep breath, he broke the seal, the crack sounding louder than he anticipated in the stillness of his dimly lit room. Inside, he found a single sheet of parchment, its edges frayed and the ink slightly smudged. As he read the words, they took shape in his mind like a long-forgotten dream coming back into focus.

"You are the last of the line. The key to unlocking the truth of your heritage lies within the shadows of the past. Seek the Crown of Eldoria before those who would silence you do so for good."

His pulse quickened. Last of the line? Crown of Eldoria? This was beyond absurd—this was a script straight out of a fantasy novel. Yet, something in his gut twisted, a nagging feeling that this wasn't just some wild tale. Daniel's phone buzzed, snapping him back to reality. It was a message from his best friend, Jake, asking if he was still coming over. The two had planned a gaming marathon to distract themselves from the mundane. But could he shake off the growing sense of dread that crept into his thoughts? He quickly typed a response, but his fingers hesitated over the screen. Should he tell Jake about the letter? Would he think he was losing his mind? Instead, he opted for a simple, "Yeah, I'll be there soon."

Tucking the letter into his pocket, he stood up, glancing at the mirror. He barely recognized the person staring back at him—tired eyes and unkempt hair. He needed to clean himself up, to prepare for the evening ahead, but the allure of the letter gnawed at him. As he walked out of his room, the world outside felt different, charged with a new energy. He reached for the door handle but paused, the weight of the letter pulling at his thoughts. What did it mean? Who was behind it? And why him? Determined to dismiss the unease, he opened the door and stepped into the hallway. But as he made his way down the stairs, a shadow flickered at the edge of his vision. He turned sharply, heart pounding, but found only the darkened corners of his home staring back at him. Brushing it off as his imagination, Daniel continued downstairs. Jake would be waiting, and maybe a few hours of gaming would clear his head. He reached the front door, pulling it open, when he heard it—a faint rustle behind him. It was soft, almost imperceptible, but it sent chills down his spine.

"Hello?" he called, his voice trembling slightly. Silence answered him, thick and suffocating.

A fleeting thought crossed his mind: what if the letter wasn't just a crazy coincidence? What if someone was already after him, someone who knew the truth? He glanced back into the house, uncertainty gnawing at him. But just as quickly, he shook it off, deciding it was best to put the mystery aside for now. He stepped out into the cool evening air, leaving the ominous feeling behind—or so he hoped. The streets were quiet as Daniel made his way to Jake's house. The soft glow of streetlights cast long shadows on the pavement, and a light breeze rustled the leaves in the trees lining the sidewalk. He tried to shake the image of the letter from his mind, but its words echoed in his thoughts like a haunting melody.

"Last of the line." What did that even mean? His family had never mentioned anything about royal connections. All he knew was his life had been typical—school, friends, the occasional family drama—but nothing that hinted at a hidden legacy. The thought both thrilled and terrified him.

He quickened his pace, wanting to drown out his thoughts with video games and laughter. But the atmosphere felt charged, as if the world held its breath. The rustling behind him returned, more pronounced this time, and he glanced over his shoulder. Nothing. Just the empty street, but the unsettling feeling remained. Arriving at Jake's house, he knocked on the door, but his mind lingered on the letter, as if it were a ghostly presence following him. Jake answered quickly, his face lighting up with enthusiasm. "Finally! I thought you were going to ditch me for a date or something."

"Yeah, right," Daniel replied, forcing a smile as he stepped inside. "Just got caught up with some... stuff."

Jake raised an eyebrow, but Daniel waved it off, not wanting to get into the letter just yet. They settled into the living room, controllers in hand, and soon the chaotic sounds of the game filled the air. But even amidst the excitement, Daniel couldn't shake the feeling that something was off. As they played, Daniel found himself distracted, his mind wandering back to the letter. The shadows in his house felt heavier, as if they were alive, waiting for him to uncover their secrets. He tried to engage with Jake, laughing at their virtual mishaps, but the laughter felt hollow, echoing in the back of his mind.

"Dude, are you even here?" Jake said, pausing the game. "You've been staring at the screen for like five minutes."

"Yeah, sorry," Daniel said, rubbing his temples. "Just... tired, I guess."

Jake studied him for a moment, then shrugged it off. "Alright, but if you're going to be all moody, I'm kicking you out."

Daniel chuckled, grateful for the distraction, but as the game resumed, he couldn't help but glance at the clock. Hours passed, the room filled with banter and laughter, yet the shadows of his unease lingered. It wasn't until they took a break that Daniel's phone buzzed again. He picked it up, heart racing. A new message had arrived, but it wasn't from Jake. Instead, it was a notification from an unknown number, containing a single line: "They know you're looking. Don't trust anyone."

Panic surged through him. Who was "they"? And how did they know about the letter? He felt a cold sweat forming on his brow as he turned to Jake, who was munching on chips, blissfully unaware of the storm brewing in Daniel's mind.

"Hey, you alright?" Jake asked, noticing Daniel's sudden shift in demeanor.

"Yeah, just... a weird message," Daniel replied, trying to keep his voice steady.

"From who?" Jake asked, curiosity piqued.

"Some random number," Daniel said, deciding to keep it vague. "Probably just spam."

Jake shrugged. "You know, you shouldn't let that stuff get to you. Just focus on the game."

Nodding, Daniel forced himself to return to the console, but the gnawing anxiety wouldn't leave him. He was in over his head, caught in a situation he didn't understand. Was it all tied to the letter? Was someone really watching him? As they resumed their game, the atmosphere felt different, electric with unspoken tension. The sense of foreboding hung heavy, and Daniel's eyes darted around the room, half-expecting someone to appear in the shadows. Hours passed, and Daniel felt a growing need to return home. The unease settled deeper in his chest, whispering that he was not safe. He excused himself, telling Jake he needed to grab something from home, but as he stepped back into the night, the weight of uncertainty pressed down harder. The streets felt eerily quiet, shadows stretching like fingers along the pavement. With every step, the feeling of being watched intensified. As he approached his home, Daniel's instincts kicked in. He felt a presence behind him, a shadow moving in the periphery of his vision. He turned quickly, but found nothing—only the stillness of the night. His heart raced as he pushed the door open, entering his home with trepidation. He flicked on the light, the brightness dispelling the darkness momentarily, but the feeling of dread settled back in as he closed the door. The letter lay heavy in his pocket, and as he pulled it out, a flicker of movement caught his eye. Outside, near the streetlamp, a figure stood, shrouded in darkness, watching. Panic surged as Daniel's heart pounded in his chest.

"Who are you?" he whispered to himself, gripping the letter tightly. But the figure remained still, unyielding, a statue in the night.

He couldn't ignore it any longer. This was bigger than he thought—bigger than some strange letter. Someone was out there, someone who knew his name, his lineage, and perhaps even his destiny. With his heart racing, Daniel took a step back, realizing that his life was about to change forever.

Chapter 2: Unwelcome Shadows

The following morning, Daniel woke to the unsettling weight of the previous night still pressing on him. The figure outside his house. The cryptic letter. The anonymous message on his phone. Sleep had been a fleeting visitor, each hour interrupted by dreams too vivid, too close to reality. Pulling himself out of bed, Daniel walked over to his window. The world outside looked deceptively normal. The morning sun filtered through the trees, casting soft light onto the quiet suburban street. No dark figures. No signs of last night's tension. It was as if the world was pretending nothing had changed, when everything had. His eyes drifted back to the letter sitting on his desk, its ancient parchment now creased from where he'd folded and unfolded it a dozen times. The Crown of Eldoria. What was that supposed to mean? And why him? He sighed, rubbing his face. He needed answers, but where to even start? Downstairs, his mom was already bustling around the kitchen, humming softly to herself. The smell of coffee and scrambled eggs filled the air, but it did little to shake Daniel from his haze.

"Morning, honey," she greeted him, her voice cheerful, completely unaware of the storm raging inside him. "I made you breakfast. You'll need your strength for today."

Daniel grabbed a mug, trying to feign normalcy. "Yeah, thanks."

As he sat at the table, his eyes wandered to the family photos lining the walls. His parents. Him as a toddler. Their vacations. All of it felt suddenly detached from reality. Could it be true—was there really a hidden part of his family's history, something they had never told him?

He wanted to ask, to demand the truth, but how could he even phrase it?

Hey, Mom, am I secretly royalty from a forgotten kingdom?

His mom sat down across from him, her bright smile faltering as she noticed his troubled expression. "You okay, Daniel? You've been a bit off since last night. Something bothering you?"

He hesitated, toying with the edge of his mug. This was it. He could bring it up now. He could show her the letter and get her reaction. Maybe she'd laugh, tell him it was some kind of prank, and the whole thing could be over.

Instead, he mumbled, "Just didn't sleep well. Weird dreams."

His mom frowned. "Well, try not to worry too much. You've always had a vivid imagination, even when you were little." She reached over and squeezed his hand. "But if something's really bothering you, you can always talk to me."

The sincerity in her voice made him feel guilty. He wasn't ready to involve her in whatever this was. Not yet.

"I know. I'm fine," he lied, forcing a smile. "I'll be fine."

As soon as breakfast was over, Daniel rushed back upstairs, pulled out his laptop, and sat down at his desk. He stared at the blank search bar, the cursor blinking back at him. What was he even supposed to type? Crown of Eldoria? Forgotten royal family? His fingers hovered over the keys before typing "Eldoria Crown" into the search bar. The results were less than helpful. Some obscure fantasy books, a historical fiction novel, a tourist site about medieval crowns—nothing that seemed remotely linked to his reality. He tried different combinations of words—Eldoria history, royal bloodline, forgotten monarchies—but every result was a dead end. Frustration simmered beneath the surface, but Daniel couldn't let it go. Something about the letter felt real, too real to ignore. His phone vibrated on the desk, snapping him out of his thoughts. Another message. He braced himself before glancing at the screen.

"Still looking, aren't you? Watch your back. They know."

Daniel's heart skipped a beat. The unknown number again. The same cryptic tone. His fingers hovered over the reply button, but what would he even say? Instead, he set the phone down, trying to control his racing thoughts. Was he being watched? Who were they? And how much did they really know about him? He needed to get out of the house. Sitting here with no answers was driving him insane. He grabbed his jacket and slipped the letter into his pocket before heading downstairs. He had to go somewhere, anywhere, where he could think. The town library wasn't far from his house, and Daniel found himself walking there almost on autopilot. His mind was still churning with questions as he made his way down the familiar streets. The air was crisp, the sun hanging low in the sky, but none of it registered. His world was narrowing down to the mystery of the letter and the warnings he couldn't shake. The library's old brick facade had always been a comforting sight, a quiet place where he could lose himself in books. Today, though, it felt like a place where he might finally find some answers. Inside, the familiar smell of worn pages and polished wood greeted him. He made his way to the history section, scanning the shelves for anything that might help. Medieval crowns, ancient kingdoms, forgotten royalty—none of it seemed to fit. But something kept pulling him back to one book in particular, its spine faded and barely legible.

He pulled it off the shelf, the leather cover cool under his fingers. The title, "Lineages of the Lost," was embossed in gold. It seemed promising, so he took it to a nearby table and began to flip through the pages. As he skimmed the chapters, his eyes caught on a passage about a kingdom that had vanished centuries ago—Eldoria. The text described it as a small but wealthy nation, its royal family wiped out in a mysterious coup. The treasure of Eldoria had been lost ever since, a prize for historians and treasure hunters alike. His pulse quickened as he read further. The royal family's symbol matched the one on the wax seal of his letter. The Crown of Eldoria was said to be more than just a symbol of power—it was believed to hold immense value, both material and... something else, something the text left vague. Daniel's hands trembled as he closed the book. This wasn't just a coincidence. The letter wasn't some prank. There really was a forgotten kingdom. And somehow, he was connected to it. He leaned back in his chair, staring blankly at the rows of books around him. What had his family been hiding all these years? And why was he only learning about this now?

A soft creak broke his concentration. Daniel looked up, startled to see a man standing near the end of the aisle. His gaze was cold, piercing, and Daniel felt the air around him shift. The man wore a long coat, his hands tucked casually in his pockets, but there was something off about him, something too calculated. Without thinking, Daniel closed the book and stood up, clutching it to his chest. The man's eyes never left him. Daniel's heart raced. Was this one of them? The mysterious they from the texts? Or was this just some stranger who happened to be in the wrong place at the wrong time? He edged around the table, keeping his eyes on the man. The stranger's expression remained unreadable, but Daniel could feel the weight of his gaze as he moved. There was no way this was a coincidence. Someone was following him. Quickening his pace, Daniel made his way toward the library's exit, his mind racing. Whoever that man was, he wasn't just a passerby. He had been watching him. And he had no idea how far they were willing to go to stop him. As Daniel stepped outside, he felt a sudden tug on his sleeve. Turning around, he came face to face with the stranger.

Chapter 3: The Stranger's Warning

The moment Daniel felt the tug on his sleeve, time seemed to slow down. He spun around, his pulse thundering in his ears, coming face to face with the man from the library. Up close, the stranger was even more imposing. He had sharp, angular features, dark stubble along his jawline, and eyes that seemed to hold more shadows than the evening sky.

"Don't run," the man said, his voice low, almost a whisper, as if the two of them were the only people in the world at that moment.

Daniel's instincts screamed at him to run, to tear away and bolt for safety. But something in the man's tone—a mixture of urgency and warning—kept him rooted to the spot.

"Who are you?" Daniel's voice cracked, betraying the fear that clenched at his chest.

The man's grip loosened slightly, but he didn't let go. He glanced around the quiet street before leaning in closer. "Not here. It's not safe."

Daniel's heart raced. "What are you talking about? What's not safe?"

The man's gaze flickered over Daniel's shoulder, scanning the street behind him. "They're watching. If we stay here, they'll find you."

They. That word again. Daniel's skin crawled. Whoever this man was, he knew more than he was letting on, and Daniel didn't trust him—yet. But the look in the man's eyes wasn't hostile. If anything, it was fear that clouded his expression. Without waiting for Daniel's consent, the man turned and started walking briskly toward the alley beside the library. "Follow me. We don't have much time."

Daniel hesitated, torn between his instinct to flee and the possibility that this stranger could provide answers. But as he glanced around the street—empty save for the creeping shadows of the setting sun—he felt exposed. If they were really watching, standing out here was a mistake. Against his better judgment, Daniel followed.

The alley was narrow and dimly lit, its cobblestone floor slick from an earlier rain. The moment they entered, the man pressed his back against the wall, casting a glance toward the street as if expecting someone to appear at any moment.

"Alright," Daniel said, his voice shaking slightly. "What's going on? Who are you, and why are you following me?"

The man studied him for a moment, then reached into his coat and pulled out a small envelope. It was nearly identical to the one Daniel had received the night before—yellowed, sealed with crimson wax, and bearing the same symbol.

"I'm not your enemy," the man said, holding out the letter. "But you need to understand what you've stepped into. They've known about you for a long time. The moment you opened that first letter, you became a target."

Daniel's mind raced. "Who? Who's after me?"

"The Order," the man replied grimly. "They've been after your family's bloodline for generations. You're the last one left, and they know it. If they catch you before you find the Crown, they'll—"

"Stop," Daniel cut him off, raising his hands in frustration. "The Crown of Eldoria, the Order—this sounds insane! I don't even know if any of this is real."

The man's jaw clenched. "I know it's overwhelming. I didn't believe it either when I was pulled into this mess. But it's real, and if you don't start believing that, you're going to end up dead."

Daniel's breath caught in his throat. The weight of the situation pressed down on him, heavier than before. "You still haven't told me who you are," he said, voice tight with suspicion.

"I'm someone who wants to keep you alive," the man said. "Name's Marcus. I've been watching your family's story for a long time."

Daniel narrowed his eyes. "Watching? Why? Who are you with?"

"I'm not with anyone," Marcus said firmly. "I used to be with the Order, but that was a long time ago. I realized what they were doing—what they wanted—and I couldn't be a part of it anymore. I left, and now I make sure people like you don't end up in their hands."

The words hung in the air between them. Daniel stared at Marcus, trying to read him. He could feel his pulse in his throat, the tension thick as the shadows around them. He wanted to believe Marcus, but how could he trust a stranger who claimed to have been part of the group hunting him?

"What do they want with me?" Daniel finally asked, his voice hoarse.

"The Order believes that whoever controls the Crown controls everything," Marcus explained. "They want the power it holds, and they believe you're the key to finding it."

Daniel swallowed hard, trying to wrap his mind around the situation. He didn't want any part of this. He had never asked for this kind of responsibility. All he wanted was to live a normal life, hang out with his friends, finish school. But that life seemed to be slipping further away with each passing minute.

"Look," Marcus said, his voice softening, "I know this isn't what you signed up for. But the reality is, you don't have a choice. The moment you opened that letter, you became part of this."

Daniel rubbed his temples, his head spinning. He wanted to believe it was all some elaborate hoax, a mistake, but the fear gnawing at his gut told him otherwise.

"I don't even know where to start," Daniel muttered.

Marcus hesitated before stepping closer. "You're not alone in this, Daniel. I can help you. But you need to trust me."

Daniel's eyes flickered to the letter still clutched in Marcus's hand. He felt the weight of his own letter in his pocket, the same seal, the same cryptic message. It was undeniable now—this was real, and it wasn't going away.

"Where do we go from here?" Daniel asked, his voice barely above a whisper.

Marcus's expression hardened. "First, you need to disappear."

Daniel blinked. "Disappear? What do you mean?"

Marcus stepped back, glancing toward the entrance of the alley again. "The Order isn't just a small group. They've got people everywhere—eyes in places you wouldn't expect. If you stay in your house, in this town, they'll find you. You need to leave, change your routine, go underground until we figure out our next move."

Daniel's pulse quickened again. Leave his life behind? His house, his friends, his mom? How was he supposed to explain that? He could feel the edges of his reality crumbling, the normalcy of his life slipping further from his grasp. The thought of disappearing, of living in the shadows, made his stomach twist.

"I can't just... vanish," Daniel stammered. "What about my family? What about school?"

Marcus's gaze softened for a moment, as if he understood the enormity of what he was asking. "I get it. This is a lot. But staying means putting everyone you love at risk. If the Order gets to you, they'll use anyone they can to force you to cooperate."

Daniel felt his throat tighten. The thought of someone hurting his mom because of him—because of whatever this Crown of Eldoria was—made him feel sick. But the idea of leaving everything behind seemed impossible.

"How do I know I can trust you?" Daniel asked, his voice low.

Marcus took a deep breath. "You don't. But I'm the only one standing between you and the people who want you dead. I was part of the Order. I know how they work, what they'll do to get what they want. If you stay, they'll find you. And once they do, it's over."

Daniel's chest tightened, the weight of Marcus's words pressing down on him. Everything in his life—his home, his friends, his plans—seemed small now, insignificant in the face of this new reality. But what choice did he have? His hand instinctively went to the letter in his pocket. The seal, the symbol—this was his family's history, his legacy, whether he wanted it or not. And now, it was his responsibility to protect it.

"Okay," Daniel finally said, his voice trembling with the gravity of his decision. "What do we do next?"

Marcus's face hardened with determination. "Pack light. We're leaving tonight."

Daniel's world was about to change forever. The question was, could he survive it?

Chapter 4: Into the Unknown

The house was quiet as Daniel packed. Too quiet. His hands moved methodically, folding clothes, stuffing his backpack with essentials: a change of clothes, his toothbrush, his phone charger. He tossed in the letter, now crinkled from being unfolded and examined too many times. His mind still swirled with uncertainty. How had his life flipped upside down in less than 24 hours? As he moved through the motions, his thoughts kept drifting to his mom. She was out, likely grocery shopping or at a friend's house, unaware that her son was about to vanish from her life with no explanation. How could he possibly tell her? How could he leave without at least trying to explain? But Marcus's warning echoed in his head: They'll use anyone to get to you. His mom wasn't safe if he stayed. He had to leave, even if it felt like the hardest thing he'd ever done. With his bag zipped and slung over his shoulder, Daniel made his way downstairs. Each step felt heavy, each creak of the wooden floor beneath him an unsettling reminder that this might be the last time he walked through this house for a long time. Maybe ever. He stood by the front door for a long moment, staring at the family photos on the wall. A picture of him and his mom on vacation, smiling in front of the beach. Another of him as a toddler, perched on his dad's shoulders before his father had passed away. These photos, these memories—they were his entire world. And now, he was about to leave it behind. His phone buzzed in his pocket, and he pulled it out to see a message from Marcus:

"I'm outside. Are you ready?"

Daniel glanced back at the kitchen, at the spot where his mom always sat with her coffee in the morning, before taking a deep breath.

There was no turning back now. He opened the door, letting the cool night air wash over him. The street was quiet, the only sound the faint rustling of leaves in the breeze. Across the street, in the shadow of an oak tree, Marcus stood waiting, arms crossed and eyes scanning the area. Daniel hesitated for a second, his heart pounding, before stepping out and closing the door behind him. With that simple act, his old life was officially over. Marcus didn't speak as Daniel approached, just gave a quick nod before turning and walking toward a parked car a few houses down. Daniel followed, feeling the weight of every step as if the air around him had thickened. When they reached the car, Marcus opened the passenger door and gestured for Daniel to get in. As soon as the door shut, Marcus slid into the driver's seat and started the engine. The hum of the car filled the silence, and they pulled away from the curb without a word. For several minutes, they drove through the darkened streets of the neighborhood. Daniel watched the familiar houses pass by, the occasional flicker of a porch light or the faint glow of a TV from someone's living room. Everything looked so normal, so mundane. But beneath the surface, a storm was brewing, and Daniel was at the center of it.

Finally, unable to stand the silence any longer, he spoke. "Where are we going?"

Marcus's eyes remained fixed on the road. "Out of town. Somewhere they won't think to look for you."

"And how long do I have to stay hidden?" Daniel asked, his voice tight with uncertainty.

"As long as it takes," Marcus replied, his tone grim. "Until we know exactly what we're up against."

Daniel slumped back in his seat, staring out the window. He had no idea what he'd just gotten himself into, and every moment seemed to raise more questions than answers. "You still haven't told me why they want me," Daniel said, turning to face Marcus. "What makes me so important?"

Marcus glanced at him briefly before returning his gaze to the road. "It's not just you they're after. It's your bloodline."

"My bloodline?" Daniel frowned. "What does that even mean?"

"Your family descends from Eldoria's royal line," Marcus explained. "The Order believes that the last surviving member of the royal family—you—is the key to finding the Crown. And with the Crown comes power. A power they've been after for centuries."

Daniel shook his head. "But I don't know anything about a crown or a kingdom. I didn't even know about Eldoria until last night."

"That's how the Order operates," Marcus said, his voice laced with bitterness. "They thrive in secrecy, manipulating history, keeping families like yours in the dark. But now that you know, they'll stop at nothing to get to you."

Daniel felt a chill run down his spine. "What does the Crown even do? Why is it so important?"

Marcus's jaw tightened. "There are stories—myths—about the Crown of Eldoria. Some say it holds the power to control nations, to bend people's will. Others say it's cursed, that whoever wears it is doomed. But the Order doesn't care about the risks. They only care about the power it promises."

The car fell silent again as Daniel processed this new information. His family—his bloodline—was connected to something ancient, something dangerous. And now, he was being hunted because of it.

"I still don't understand why me," Daniel said quietly. "I'm nobody special."

Marcus shot him a sideways glance. "That's exactly why they want you. Because you don't know what you're capable of."

They drove for nearly two hours before the landscape began to change. The urban sprawl of the city gradually gave way to winding roads and dense forests. The moon hung low in the sky, casting pale light over the trees as they ventured deeper into the countryside. Eventually, Marcus turned off the main road and onto a narrow, gravel path that wound its way through the trees. The car bounced along the uneven terrain, the headlights cutting through the darkness. Daniel could feel the tension building in his chest again, an uneasy sense that they were heading toward something unknown. After what felt like an eternity, the trees thinned, revealing a small, run-down cabin nestled in the woods. Its windows were dark, the wooden siding weathered and worn. It didn't look like much, but something about it felt safe—hidden.

"We'll stay here for the night," Marcus said, cutting the engine and stepping out of the car. "No one will find us here."

Daniel followed him, his shoes crunching on the gravel as he approached the cabin. The air smelled of pine and damp earth, the only sound the distant rustle of the wind in the trees. It felt a world away from his life back home. Marcus pushed open the cabin door, revealing a small, sparsely furnished interior. A single bed, a table, and a couple of chairs. It was clear this wasn't meant to be a long-term hideout, just a temporary refuge.

"You can take the bed," Marcus said, tossing his bag onto the floor. "I'll keep watch."

Daniel didn't argue. He was too exhausted, mentally and physically. As soon as he sat on the edge of the bed, his body felt like it might collapse. But sleep wouldn't come easily, not with everything that had happened, not with the uncertainty hanging over him like a storm cloud. He lay down, staring up at the ceiling, listening to the soft creak of the cabin as the wind pressed against its walls. His mind wouldn't stop racing. The Crown. The Order. His family's bloodline. None of it made sense, and yet here he was, in the middle of it all. Marcus sat by the window, his silhouette barely visible in the dim light of the moon filtering through the trees. He hadn't said much since they arrived, but Daniel could feel the man's vigilance, the way his eyes scanned the dark woods outside.

Daniel's hands clenched into fists. They were here—the Order. They'd found him, and now they were coming for him. He looked at Marcus, his mind racing. What was the plan? Were they going to run? Fight? He couldn't just sit here and wait to be dragged into whatever hell the Order had in store for him.

Marcus finally moved, his voice low but clear. "Stay inside, Daniel. No matter what happens, don't come out."

Daniel's heart pounded harder. "But—"

"Trust me," Marcus cut him off, his eyes locking onto Daniel's for the briefest of moments. "I'll handle this."

Before Daniel could protest, Marcus disappeared into the trees, melting into the shadows. The last thing Daniel saw was the gleam of the gun in Marcus's hand before the darkness swallowed him whole. Daniel's mind raced, torn between the urge to run and the instinct to stay put. But Marcus's warning echoed in his head. He had to trust him. Marcus knew these people, knew what they were capable of. But the pit in Daniel's stomach twisted tighter with each passing second, the silence outside only amplifying the fear gnawing at him. Then it happened—fast. Too fast for Daniel to process.

A gunshot rang out, shattering the stillness of the night. Daniel flinched, his heart leaping into his throat. He scrambled back from the door, his hands trembling as his mind screamed at him to run, to hide, to do anything but stay in this vulnerable spot. But his legs felt like lead, his body frozen with fear. Another gunshot followed, then a rustling of leaves—a scuffle. Someone was fighting out there, and it didn't take long for Daniel to realize who it was. His thoughts spiraled as the sounds of struggle grew more violent. What if Marcus couldn't handle this? What if the Order had sent more people? What if—

A third gunshot exploded through the night, and then—silence. The forest seemed to hold its breath. Daniel's pulse roared in his ears as he crouched by the cabin's entrance, his mind reeling. He wanted to rush outside, to help, to find Marcus, but fear pinned him in place.

What if it wasn't over? What if the Order was still out there, waiting for him to make a move? A few agonizing seconds passed before he heard it—a soft, deliberate footstep approaching the cabin. Daniel's breath caught in his throat. He backed away from the door, his heart racing. The footsteps grew louder, closer. Whoever was outside was coming for him now. Suddenly, the door swung open, and Marcus stepped into the cabin, his chest heaving with shallow breaths. His clothes were damp with sweat, his gun still in his hand, but his eyes burned with determination.

"It's done," he said, his voice rough and strained.

Daniel swallowed hard. "Are they—?"

"Gone." Marcus's expression was grim, his eyes betraying the tension still coursing through him. "But more will come. We need to move."

Without waiting for a response, Marcus strode across the cabin, yanking open a small cupboard in the corner. He pulled out a set of maps and began spreading them out on the table, his movements swift and efficient. "There's a safe house about thirty miles from here, deeper in the woods. It's more secure than this place. We'll head there tonight."

Daniel hesitated, his mind still reeling from what had just happened. "Who were they?" he asked, his voice barely above a whisper.

Marcus didn't look up from the maps. "Operatives from the Order. They track people like us—people who know too much."

Daniel felt a chill crawl up his spine. "Did they... did they know I was here?"

Marcus's jaw tightened. "Not yet. They were after me. But it's only a matter of time before they realize you're involved. That's why we need to leave. Now."

Daniel stood frozen for a moment, the weight of everything crashing down on him. His life was slipping further away with each passing second, and he didn't know how to stop it. He didn't know if he even wanted to stop it. But one thing was clear: staying here was no longer an option.

He moved toward the door, his body numb with exhaustion and fear. "What happens next?" he asked, his voice shaking.

Marcus folded the maps and stuffed them into his bag. "We disappear. For good, if necessary."

The finality of those words hit Daniel like a punch to the gut. Disappear. Was that really what his life had come to? Running, hiding, never looking back? The idea of leaving everything behind—his mom, his friends, his home—felt like a nightmare he couldn't wake up from.

But Marcus's voice broke through his thoughts, sharp and commanding. "Get your things. We're leaving in five."

Daniel nodded, his throat tight. He grabbed his backpack, which now felt impossibly small for the weight of the journey ahead, and slung it over his shoulder. The cabin that had once seemed like a refuge now felt like a prison, suffocating and cold. As he stepped outside into the crisp night air, he glanced over at Marcus, who was already scanning the treeline, ever watchful, ever prepared. There was no trace of the warmth or camaraderie that Daniel had hoped might develop between them. Marcus was a soldier, and this was a mission. Nothing more. The car was still parked by the edge of the clearing, its headlights dim as they climbed in. The night around them felt heavier now, the shadows deeper, as if the trees themselves were closing in, waiting for the next move.

Marcus started the engine, his eyes flicking to the rearview mirror. "We'll drive as far as we can tonight. I'll explain more when we reach the safe house."

Daniel didn't respond. He stared out the window, watching as the trees blurred past, his mind spinning with questions that seemed to have no answers. Hours passed in silence, the road winding through endless stretches of forest, the occasional glimpse of a distant farmhouse or a flicker of headlights from another car. Daniel felt the exhaustion creeping in, his eyelids growing heavier with each passing mile. But sleep wouldn't come. Not with the weight of everything that had happened, not with the uncertainty of what lay ahead. Finally, Marcus broke the silence.

"There's something you need to understand," he said, his voice low. "The Order isn't just after the Crown. They're after you because of what you represent. You're the last of your family's bloodline, the last legitimate heir to the throne of Eldoria."

Daniel blinked, trying to process the words. "What... what does that even mean? I'm just a kid. I don't know anything about thrones or crowns."

Marcus's eyes flicked to him for a brief second before returning to the road. "Your family has kept secrets for centuries. Secrets about the Crown, about Eldoria, about the true power it holds. The Order wants that power. And they'll stop at nothing to get it."

Daniel felt his heart race again. "But I don't know anything. I don't know where the Crown is or how to find it."

"That's why they need you," Marcus said, his voice grim. "Because whether you know it or not, your blood holds the key to unlocking its location."

Daniel's head spun. None of this made sense, but he couldn't deny the fear that was now a permanent knot in his chest. "What if I don't want to find the
Crown?"

Marcus's lips pressed into a thin line. "It's not about what you want anymore. It's about survival."

As Marcus's words hung in the air, the sound of a car engine roared to life behind them, headlights flooding the rearview mirror. Someone was following them.

Chapter 6: The Pursuit

The blinding headlights filled the rearview mirror, and Daniel's heart jumped into his throat. His hands instinctively tightened around the edges of his seat as the low growl of the car engine behind them grew louder, closer. Marcus cursed under his breath, his eyes narrowing as he slammed his foot down on the gas. The car lurched forward, the tires squealing against the asphalt as they sped through the narrow forest road. Daniel felt his body press into the seat, adrenaline surging through him like electricity.

"They found us," Marcus muttered, his voice strained with frustration.

Daniel glanced over his shoulder. The car tailing them was no longer a shadow in the distance. It was gaining, fast. Panic clawed at his chest. "What do we do now?"

Marcus's jaw tightened. "Hold on."

Without warning, Marcus jerked the wheel to the left, the car skidding as it veered off the main road and onto a dirt trail. The sudden turn sent a cloud of dust billowing up behind them, momentarily obscuring the view of their pursuers. Daniel's stomach lurched as the car bounced violently over the uneven terrain. The headlights behind them wavered but didn't disappear. Whoever was chasing them wasn't going to give up easily. The road twisted and turned, the dense trees on either side creating a tunnel of darkness that made it hard to see more than a few feet ahead. Every bump, every jolt sent Daniel's heart racing faster. He could barely breathe, the fear gnawing at his insides like a living thing. Marcus's face was a mask of concentration, his hands gripping the wheel so tightly that his knuckles were white. He didn't speak, but the tension radiating off him was palpable. Daniel could tell that this was no ordinary pursuit. Whoever was behind them knew exactly what they were after.

"Can we outrun them?" Daniel asked, his voice barely audible over the roar of the engine.

"We don't have a choice," Marcus replied through gritted teeth. "But this trail won't last forever. If they catch us before we reach the safe house—"

He didn't finish the sentence, but the implication was clear. Daniel turned to look out the back window again. The headlights were still there, relentless and unyielding. His mind raced, trying to think of something—anything—that could help them. But he was no strategist. He wasn't a fighter. He was just a kid caught up in something far bigger than he could ever understand. Suddenly, the road ahead opened up into a clearing, and Marcus seized the opportunity. He yanked the wheel hard to the right, sending the car careening off the dirt trail and into the thick underbrush. The vehicle crashed through branches and shrubs, the sound of breaking wood and scraping metal filling the air. Daniel's body jerked violently as the car jolted over the uneven ground. He clenched his teeth, trying to keep from being thrown around in the seat. His heart pounded in his ears, every second stretching out into what felt like an eternity. The headlights disappeared as they plunged deeper into the woods. But the reprieve was temporary. Marcus killed the engine, the car coming to a skidding halt behind a thick wall of trees. He motioned for Daniel to stay silent, and for a moment, all Daniel could hear was the sound of his own ragged breathing. The pursuers were close—too close. Daniel could hear the faint hum of their engine as they slowed down, searching for their trail. His heart threatened to burst out of his chest as he held his breath, waiting for the inevitable. Minutes passed, each one heavier than the last. Daniel's muscles ached from the tension, his eyes fixed on Marcus, waiting for a signal. But Marcus remained still, his gaze locked on the tree line, listening.

Finally, the sound of the engine faded, and Daniel let out a shaky breath. "Did we lose them?"

Marcus's face remained hard. "For now."

Daniel slumped back in his seat, the relief fleeting. They might have escaped for the moment, but it was clear that this was only the beginning. He couldn't shake the feeling that whoever was chasing them wouldn't stop until they got what they wanted.

"Who are they?" Daniel asked after a long silence. "Are they from the Order?"

Marcus hesitated before nodding. "Yes. They're the Order's enforcers. The ones they send when they want to eliminate a threat quickly."

Daniel's blood ran cold. "Eliminate?"

"They don't want you alive, Daniel," Marcus said bluntly. "Not after what you've learned. Not after what you could become."

Daniel swallowed hard, his throat dry. "What do you mean, what I could become?"

Marcus turned to face him, his eyes dark and unreadable. "You're the last heir of the Eldorian bloodline, Daniel. That means you're more than just a kid caught in the wrong place at the wrong time. You have the potential to reclaim the throne, to take back the power that was stolen from your family centuries ago."

Daniel blinked, struggling to process the weight of Marcus's words. "But... I don't want that. I don't even know what that means."

Marcus's gaze softened, but only slightly. "It doesn't matter what you want. The Order sees you as a threat because of what you could become. They've spent generations trying to wipe out the last traces of your family, and now that you're the only one left, they're not going to stop until you're gone."

Daniel's mind spun. He wasn't royalty. He wasn't destined for anything great. He was just a teenager who'd stumbled into something far bigger than he could handle. But as he looked into Marcus's eyes, he realized there was no escaping this now. Whether he wanted it or not, his life had changed forever.

"We're not far from the safe house," Marcus said, breaking the silence. "We'll lie low there for a while. Regroup, figure out our next move."

Daniel nodded numbly, his thoughts swirling with confusion and fear. He didn't know what to believe anymore. Everything Marcus had told him felt like a nightmare—a twisted fantasy that had somehow become his reality. But as much as he wanted to deny it, there was no escaping the truth. They were in danger. And the Order was coming for him. Marcus restarted the car, driving slowly through the thick forest, careful to avoid making too much noise. The tension between them was thick, unspoken but palpable. Daniel stared out the window, watching as the trees blurred past, his mind racing with questions he wasn't sure he wanted the answers to. After what felt like hours, the car finally pulled up to a small, unassuming cabin nestled deep in the woods. It looked abandoned, with overgrown vines crawling up the sides and broken shutters hanging loosely from the windows. But there was a sense of security about it, like it had been built to withstand more than just the elements.

"We'll be safe here," Marcus said as he cut the engine. "At least for a little while."

Daniel nodded, though he wasn't entirely convinced. He followed Marcus out of the car, his eyes scanning the surrounding woods for any signs of movement. The silence was unsettling, like the calm before a storm. Marcus unlocked the cabin door and stepped inside, motioning for Daniel to follow. The interior was sparse but functional—a single room with a bed, a small table, and a wood-burning stove. There were no luxuries here, no comforts. This was a place to hide, not to live.

Marcus dropped his bag onto the floor and immediately began checking the windows, securing the locks and drawing the heavy curtains shut. Daniel stood awkwardly by the door, unsure of what to do next.

"What happens now?" Daniel asked, his voice small in the quiet space.

Marcus turned to him, his expression unreadable. "Now we wait. And we plan."

Daniel opened his mouth to ask what they were planning for, but before he could speak, there was a sudden noise outside—a low rustling, followed by the sound of footsteps approaching the cabin. Both of them froze. Marcus's hand shot to his gun, his body tense and ready. The door creaked. The door slowly swings open, revealing a figure standing in the shadows.

Chapter 7: An Unexpected Ally

The door creaked open, its slow, agonizing motion making Daniel's pulse throb in his ears. The figure standing in the shadows was nothing more than a silhouette, but the sight of them sent a jolt of fear down his spine. He stepped back, his feet faltering against the rough wooden floor, as Marcus raised his gun, eyes narrowed, ready to fire. The cabin felt too small, too confined, the air thick with dread. Daniel's mind raced. Had the Order found them already? Was this it?

The figure stepped forward, their face still obscured in shadow, but their movements were deliberate, calm. They stopped just inside the doorway, hands raised slightly—a non-threatening gesture. The tension in the room stretched thin, and Daniel could hear his own shallow breathing. Time seemed to slow.

"Marcus," the figure spoke, their voice low but steady. "You can lower your weapon. I'm not here to harm you."

Marcus didn't budge, his finger hovering over the trigger. His eyes remained locked on the figure, but Daniel could see the shift in his expression—recognition, mixed with suspicion. "What are you doing here?" Marcus's voice was ice-cold, every word a warning. The figure stepped into the light, and Daniel's breath caught in his throat. It was a woman, probably in her early thirties, her dark hair pulled back into a tight braid. Her face was sharp, and angular, with high cheekbones and piercing blue eyes that seemed to take in everything at once. She was dressed in all black, her clothes practical and worn, as though she'd been traveling for days without rest.

"I came to help," she said simply, her gaze shifting briefly to Daniel before returning to Marcus.

"Help?" Marcus's voice was laced with disbelief. "Last I heard, you were done with this. With us."

The woman's lips pressed into a thin line, and for a moment, she looked almost regretful. "Things change."

Marcus lowered his gun, but only slightly. His eyes never left hers. "You're not supposed to be here. You're putting him—" he nodded toward Daniel—"in even more danger."

Daniel's pulse quickened. *Her presence puts me in more danger? Who is she?*

The woman exhaled slowly, stepping further into the cabin and closing the door behind her with a soft click. "I know what I'm risking by being here, Marcus. But I also know the stakes." She glanced at Daniel again, her expression unreadable. "He doesn't even know the half of it, does he?"

Daniel felt a pang of anger rise up alongside the fear. He hated being spoken about like he wasn't in the room, like his entire life had been reduced to a game of chess, where he was just a pawn. He stepped forward, his voice shaky but defiant. "I'm right here, you know. And I'd like to know what's going on. Who are you?"

The woman's eyes flicked to him, a hint of something—perhaps pity, perhaps respect—softening her otherwise steely gaze. "I'm someone who's been in your shoes before," she said, her tone gentler now. "My name's Evelyn. I used to work for the Order."

The revelation hit Daniel like a punch to the gut. His mind struggled to process it. Someone who worked for the Order, now standing in front of him, claiming to want to help?

Marcus's jaw tightened. "You were their top operative, Evelyn. Why should I trust you now?"

Evelyn's eyes flashed, and for the first time, Daniel saw the fire behind her calm exterior. "Because I walked away. I walked away when I realized what the Order truly was—what they were willing to do to people like him." She motioned to Daniel, her voice hardening. "They don't just want the Crown, Marcus. They want to destroy everything tied to the old royal bloodlines. And that includes him. They'll wipe out anyone who stands in their way."

Daniel's mouth went dry. "But why? Why are they so desperate to erase everything?"

Evelyn looked at him, her gaze piercing. "Because the Crown isn't just a symbol. It holds power. Real, tangible power. The kind that can change everything—the kind that can control nations, and rewrite histories. And your family, the royal bloodline you carry, is the key to unlocking that power. The Order knows it. That's why they've hunted down every last descendant. And that's why they'll never stop until they have you."

Daniel felt like the ground had been ripped out from under him. His entire life, he'd been just an ordinary teenager. Or so he'd thought. Now, he was being told that he was the last piece in some ancient, deadly puzzle that could reshape the world.

"How do I even fit into this?" Daniel asked, his voice barely above a whisper. "I don't know anything about this 'power.' I've never even heard of it."

Evelyn's gaze softened slightly. "You don't need to understand it yet. But trust me when I say that the Order does. They've been working for decades, centuries even, to get their hands on it. And they're closer now than they've ever been. The only thing standing between them and total control is you."

Marcus stepped forward, his eyes flicking back and forth between Daniel and Evelyn. His expression was one of barely contained frustration. "And why should we believe you, Evelyn? You walked away from the Order, sure. But that doesn't mean you're on our side."

Evelyn's jaw clenched, and she stepped closer to Marcus, her voice dropping to a near whisper. "Because I know what's coming, Marcus. I know their next move. I've seen the files. They're mobilizing an entire team—elites, assassins. They're sending them here, to this region, to hunt you both down. If you don't leave this cabin now, tonight, they'll find you. And when they do, there won't be any running."

Daniel's heart thudded in his chest. "They're coming here? How do you know?"

Evelyn looked at him with a steady, unwavering gaze. "Because I was supposed to be leading that team."

The room fell into an icy silence, the weight of her words sinking in. Daniel's mind raced, trying to make sense of everything she had said. He felt trapped, not just by the looming threat of the Order, but by the tangled web of secrets and lies that seemed to be closing in around him.

Marcus broke the silence, his voice low and dangerous. "You're telling me they'll be here tonight? And that you just decided to show up now, after all these years, to warn us?"

Evelyn's expression hardened. "I didn't come here for your gratitude, Marcus. I came because whether you like it or not, you need me if you want to survive. I know how they operate. I know how they think. And right now, you're both sitting ducks."

Daniel's pulse quickened. The air in the cabin felt thick and oppressive. Every instinct screamed at him to run, but there was nowhere to go. Not yet. He glanced between Marcus and Evelyn, trying to read the tension between them. It was clear they had a history, and it wasn't a good one. But that didn't change the fact that Evelyn's warning felt real. Too real.

"What do we do?" Daniel asked, his voice trembling despite his best efforts to stay calm.

Evelyn met his gaze, her expression softening ever so slightly. "We leave. Now. There's a network of safe houses in the region, places the Order doesn't know about. If we move fast, we can get to one before they track us here."

Marcus folded his arms, his gaze hard and skeptical. "And how do I know this isn't some elaborate trap? You could be leading us right into their hands."

Evelyn's eyes flared with frustration. "If I wanted you dead, Marcus, I wouldn't have warned you. I wouldn't be standing here risking my life to get you out."

Daniel stepped forward, his voice stronger now. "We don't have a choice, Marcus. If the Order is coming, we can't stay here. Whether we trust her or not, we have to move."

Marcus's jaw tightened, and for a long moment, he stood there, silent and brooding. Finally, he nodded, his expression dark. "Fine. But if this goes south, if you're lying to us, Evelyn—"

"I'm not lying," Evelyn cut him off, her voice sharp. "But we need to go. Now."

The next few minutes were a blur of motion. Marcus packed their essentials quickly, gathering supplies with the efficiency of someone who had done this many times before. Daniel threw his few belongings into his bag, his hands shaking with adrenaline. The cabin that had once seemed like a sanctuary now felt like a death trap, its walls closing in around him. He glanced out the small, grimy window, half-expecting to see the lights of the Order's cars bearing down on them. Evelyn stood by the door, her posture tense but composed, her sharp eyes scanning the woods outside for any signs of movement. She moved with the grace of someone who had spent her life in dangerous situations, someone who knew exactly how to survive.

"Ready?" Marcus asked, his voice tight as he slung his bag over his shoulder.

Daniel nodded, though he wasn't sure he'd ever feel ready for what was coming next. Evelyn didn't wait for a response. She pushed open the door and stepped out into the night, motioning for them to follow. The air outside was cool and thick with the scent of pine and earth, but it did nothing to calm Daniel's racing heart. As they disappeared into the dark forest, leaving the cabin behind, Daniel couldn't shake the feeling that they were being watched. Every rustle of leaves, and every distant sound sent a shiver down his spine. They were running now. And Daniel knew, deep down, that the Order wasn't far behind. A distant light flickered through the trees, growing brighter with every step they took.

Chapter 8: Shadows in the Dark

The forest was silent, save for the sound of their footsteps crunching against the underbrush. Every step they took seemed louder than it should, as if the trees themselves were conspiring to give them away. The thick canopy overhead cast everything in shadow, only allowing the faintest slivers of moonlight to guide their path. Daniel's pulse raced, his senses heightened by the urgency of their flight. Beside him, Marcus moved with a predator's precision, his head swiveling constantly, scanning for any signs of pursuit. Daniel could feel the tension radiating off of him in waves. Evelyn led the way, her pace steady but unrelenting, not once looking back. She was too calm, too composed. It unnerved him.

After what felt like hours of walking, Daniel finally whispered, "Where are we going?"

Evelyn didn't break stride. "There's a cabin. Safe house. About three miles from here."

"And you're sure the Order doesn't know about it?" Marcus asked, his voice low but sharp.

"They don't," Evelyn replied confidently. "I helped set it up years ago, before I left. They haven't had eyes on it in over a decade."

Marcus grunted, clearly still not convinced, but said nothing more. Daniel swallowed hard, his thoughts swirling. He couldn't shake the feeling that they were being watched. The forest around them was thick, dark, and full of places to hide. His mind was playing tricks on him—every snapping twig or rustling leaf sent a jolt of adrenaline through his veins.

Are they already here?

He glanced at Marcus, who walked with purpose, the cold steel of his handgun still visible in his hand. The man hadn't put the weapon away since they left the cabin. Daniel wished he had something to defend himself with, but Marcus hadn't offered, and he didn't know the first thing about guns.

"So," Daniel began, trying to fill the suffocating silence, "how long have you been...on the run?"

Evelyn slowed slightly, enough that Daniel could walk closer. Her eyes stayed forward, but her voice softened, losing some of its edge. "It's been a while. I used to be part of the Order, like I said. They... groomed me for it. Recruited me when I was younger than you are now."

Daniel's stomach turned. "You didn't have a choice?"

Evelyn let out a bitter laugh. "Not much of one. They make it sound like a choice, but the truth is, once they've got their hooks in you, there's no escaping. At least, that's what I thought."

Marcus snorted quietly but didn't interrupt.

Daniel pressed on. "But you did escape. Why?"

Evelyn's face hardened again, her eyes dark as they cut through the forest ahead. "Because I realized that they weren't protecting anything. They weren't preserving history or maintaining balance like they always preached. They were hungry for power. And they'd do anything—sacrifice anyone—to get it." She glanced at Daniel, her expression grim. "Including you."

Daniel's heart pounded in his chest as the weight of Evelyn's words settled over him. *They'll sacrifice anyone... including me?* He hadn't fully grasped how deep he was in this. His entire life had felt normal up until a few weeks ago, but now it was as though he had stepped into a world he didn't understand—and the cost of being a part of it was his very existence.

"How do you know all of this?" Daniel asked, his voice quieter now, almost afraid to know the full answer.

Evelyn's eyes darkened further, the kind of expression one wears when reliving painful memories. "I wasn't always just a cog in their machine. I got promoted, eventually. I saw things, was given access to things that most people would never be allowed to see. Ancient texts, rituals... things they've been planning for centuries. The Order has roots so deep in the world's history that it's almost impossible to tell where they stop and where governments, churches, and societies begin."

She paused for a moment, stepping carefully over a fallen log as the forest thickened around them. Daniel followed closely, stumbling a little but trying to keep up. "The royal bloodline isn't just symbolic," she continued. "It's tied to something older—something dangerous. You're the last key, Daniel. The last of the bloodline they haven't gotten to."

Daniel's throat went dry. "But why me? I'm no one special. I don't know anything about royal bloodlines or power."

"That's what they want you to believe," Marcus interjected from behind, his voice a low growl. "Keeping you in the dark is part of their strategy. If you don't know your own importance, you're easier to control."

Evelyn nodded. "Exactly. And they've been very good at keeping it that way, making sure anyone tied to the old line either doesn't survive, or doesn't know what they're connected to."

Daniel felt like the ground was shifting beneath him. He couldn't reconcile the life he knew with the one Evelyn and Marcus were describing. It sounded like something out of a story, a twisted conspiracy that couldn't possibly be real—except it was. He was living it now. The fear of being hunted, the endless questions about his own family, the lies that had been built around him—it all made sense in the most terrifying way.

"How much further?" Marcus asked, his voice snapping Daniel out of his spiraling thoughts.

Evelyn glanced around, eyes narrowing as she scanned the trees. "Not far. A little over a mile, but we need to keep moving. We're exposed out here."

The sense of being watched gnawed at Daniel's nerves. He glanced over his shoulder, the shadows behind them shifting with the wind. Were they really alone? Or was the Order already on their trail, watching from a distance, waiting for the right moment to strike?

"Do you hear that?" Evelyn suddenly stopped, her hand raised, signaling silence.

The three of them froze. Daniel strained to listen, but at first, all he could hear was the rustling of leaves in the night breeze, the faint sound of distant animals stirring in the underbrush. Then... there it was. A soft, rhythmic crunch of footsteps, too deliberate to be wild animals. It was faint but growing closer.

Marcus's grip tightened around his gun, his eyes narrowing. "They're here."

Evelyn's expression shifted from calm to urgent, her voice dropping into a tense whisper. "We can't outrun them. They know these woods as well as we do."

Marcus cursed under his breath. "How far to the safe house?"

"Too far to risk it without being seen," Evelyn muttered. She scanned the area quickly before her eyes settled on a rocky outcropping a few hundred yards to the right, partially concealed by the dense undergrowth. "We'll hide there. Follow me."

Without waiting for a response, she darted off toward the rocks, her movements swift and silent. Marcus and Daniel followed, moving as quickly as they could while trying to stay quiet. The footsteps behind them grew louder, more distinct, confirming what they already knew—someone was closing in. They reached the rocks just as the sound of pursuit became unmistakable. Daniel pressed himself into the cold stone, his breath shallow and his heart thundering in his chest. Marcus knelt beside him, gun drawn, while Evelyn crouched a few feet away, her body tense, ready for action. The footsteps slowed, and Daniel's blood ran cold. He could hear voices now, low murmurs in a language he didn't recognize, as the figures approached. There were at least three of them, maybe more, moving methodically through the forest, searching. Evelyn's eyes met Marcus's, and without speaking, she motioned toward the figures with a quick hand signal. Marcus nodded grimly, raising his gun slightly, his finger hovering over the trigger. Daniel could barely breathe. If they were found, there was no telling what would happen. The voices grew louder, the figures drawing closer to their hiding spot. Daniel caught a glimpse of them through the leaves—dark silhouettes moving with precision, weapons gleaming faintly in the moonlight. They were trained, professional, and deadly. One of the figures stopped, turning toward the rocks where they were hidden. Daniel's heart slammed against his ribs, his muscles frozen in fear. The figure took a step closer, and Daniel's breath hitched. He could feel Marcus beside him, completely still, ready to fire at the slightest sign of discovery. The figure took another step, their gaze sweeping over the rocks. Daniel's skin prickled with dread, his mind screaming that it was over, that they were about to be caught. But then, just as the figure seemed to fix their eyes on their hiding place, one of the others called out in that same strange language. The figure hesitated, glancing back toward the others. There was a brief exchange of words before the first figure reluctantly turned away, rejoining the others. Daniel exhaled a shaky breath, his body trembling from the rush of adrenaline. The figures moved further into the forest, their footsteps growing fainter as they continued their search elsewhere. For now, they were safe.

Evelyn waited until the sound of their pursuers had faded completely before she motioned for them to move again. "Come on," she whispered. "We don't have much time."

They slipped out from behind the rocks, moving cautiously but quickly, weaving through the trees and staying low. The forest seemed quieter now, more ominous. Every sound felt amplified, and Daniel couldn't shake the feeling that they were still being watched. After what felt like an eternity of moving through the dense woods, they finally came to a clearing. In the center stood a small, nondescript cabin, nearly hidden by the surrounding trees. It was old, its wooden walls weathered by years of exposure to the elements, but it looked sturdy enough. Evelyn moved to the door and pressed her hand against a hidden panel on the side. There was a faint click, and the door swung open. She stepped inside, motioning for them to follow. Once inside, Marcus immediately moved to check the windows, securing the locks and pulling the thick curtains closed. The interior was sparse but functional—a single room with a bed, a small kitchen area, and a fireplace. There was a stack of supplies in one corner—food, water, and medical equipment, all neatly organized.

"This will hold for now," Evelyn said, her voice low but steady. "They won't be able to find us here."

Daniel collapsed into a chair, his mind racing, trying to make sense of everything that had happened. His body was exhausted, but his thoughts wouldn't stop spinning. He was no closer to understanding his place in all of this, and the fear of what was coming next gnawed at him.

Marcus sat across from him, his gun resting on the table, his expression grim. "We can't stay here for long. They'll figure out where we went sooner or later."

Evelyn nodded. "I know. But for now, we need to rest. Regain our strength."

The tension in the room was palpable, thick enough to cut with a knife. They were safe, for now, but Daniel knew that wouldn't last. The Order was relentless, and this was just the beginning. In the stillness of the night, a faint noise echoed from outside—a distant, metallic clang that made Daniel's heart skip a beat. They weren't alone.

Chapter 9: Echoes of the Past

The metallic clang echoed through the small cabin, setting Daniel's nerves on edge. He sat frozen, his eyes darting toward the door. The sound had been faint, almost distant, but unmistakable—a cold, unnatural noise that didn't belong in the quiet forest night. His pulse quickened, the hair on the back of his neck prickling with the same dread that had been creeping through him since they'd left the first cabin. Marcus was already on his feet, gun drawn, moving silently toward the door with the smooth precision of someone who'd done this a thousand times before. Evelyn's expression darkened, her gaze sharp as she followed Marcus, her hand slipping to the blade strapped to her leg. Daniel stood, unsure of what to do. His body tensed with adrenaline, but his mind raced. Every instinct screamed for him to run, but where would he go? They were in the middle of nowhere, and the Order was relentless.

Marcus peered through the narrow crack in the curtain, his movements careful, deliberate. "Nothing," he muttered, though his voice was laced with suspicion. He turned to Evelyn, his tone sharp. "You think they've found us?"

Evelyn didn't respond immediately. She moved to one of the side windows and did a quick scan of the surrounding woods. Her brow furrowed, but she shook her head. "It doesn't make sense. If they were here, we would have heard more than just one sound." She paused, eyes narrowing. "But we can't assume anything."

Daniel hovered near the center of the room, every muscle in his body tight, ready to bolt at any second. "What do we do?"

Evelyn turned back to him, her face grim. "We wait. We don't make any sudden moves. Marcus, check the perimeter."

Without a word, Marcus slipped through the back door, disappearing into the night. His figure melted into the darkness, leaving Daniel and Evelyn alone in the heavy silence. The minutes stretched on, each one feeling longer than the last. Daniel couldn't stop the thoughts that raced through his head—who was out there? Was the Order watching them, toying with them, waiting for the right moment to strike? Every creak of the old wooden cabin felt amplified, making his skin crawl with anxiety.

"You said something before," Daniel whispered, breaking the silence. "About me. About why they're after me."

Evelyn's gaze flicked to him, her eyes cautious. "You want answers now?"

"Yeah, now seems like a pretty good time for answers," Daniel shot back, the frustration clear in his voice. He was tired of being kept in the dark, tired of running without understanding what he was running from. "What do you know about me that I don't?"

Evelyn hesitated, glancing toward the door as if expecting Marcus to return at any moment. When he didn't, she finally exhaled and spoke. "You're part of something older than the Order itself. Older than any of us. Your family—the bloodline you come from—has been hunted for centuries. The royal bloodline isn't just symbolic. It's tied to something deeper. A power that they've spent generations trying to control."

Daniel blinked, his mind reeling. "A power? What kind of power?"

"The bloodline you're connected to is more than just royalty. It's part of an ancient lineage, one that has ties to abilities that people like the Order would kill to control. That's why they're after you," Evelyn said, her voice lowering as if the walls themselves might hear. "You're the last direct descendant of that line."

Daniel stared at her, the weight of her words crashing into him like a wave. "Abilities? What abilities?"

Evelyn's expression softened, but her voice was firm. "I don't know exactly. It's not something that's been fully revealed, but the Order believes that through your bloodline, they can unlock things that have been buried in history—things that could reshape the world in ways we can't imagine."

A cold shiver ran down Daniel's spine. The words felt like they belonged in a nightmare, not his life. But there was something about the way Evelyn spoke, something in her eyes that made him realize she wasn't exaggerating. She believed every word.

"So, what... they want to use me? To activate this... power?"

"Yes," Evelyn said flatly. "That's why they've been keeping tabs on your family for so long. Your parents knew, I think. That's why they went off the grid."

The mention of his parents felt like a punch to the gut. Daniel's breath caught, and for a moment, the entire room seemed to spin. He hadn't thought about his parents like that—hadn't connected their disappearance with something this enormous. He'd assumed they'd left him, but what if they hadn't? What if they were running, hiding him from something far worse?

"But why didn't they tell me?" he asked, his voice tight with emotion. "Why didn't they warn me about any of this?"

Evelyn's expression softened, her eyes full of empathy. "They were trying to protect you. The less you knew, the safer you were. The Order can't manipulate someone who doesn't know the truth. It's how they've stayed one step ahead of them all these years."

Daniel clenched his fists, the frustration and confusion swirling in him like a storm. "And now what? Am I just supposed to accept this? That my life has been some kind of... setup for something I don't even understand?"

Before Evelyn could answer, the back door swung open, and Marcus slipped inside. His face was set in a grim line, his gun still in hand.

"They're gone," Marcus muttered, glancing at Evelyn. "But they were here."

Evelyn frowned. "What do you mean?"

"I found tracks, faint but recent. At least two of them, maybe three. They were circling us, probably scoping out the cabin." He glanced around the room, his jaw clenched. "They know we're here. It's only a matter of time before they come back."

Daniel's heart sank. There was no escaping this, was there? They would always be one step behind, always chasing shadows until the Order caught up with them.

"We can't stay here," Marcus continued. "We need to move before they regroup."

Evelyn didn't hesitate. "There's another safe house, about thirty miles north. But we'll need to be careful. The deeper we go, the more their influence spreads."

Marcus nodded, his expression serious. "We leave now."

Daniel's stomach churned. Thirty miles? They had barely escaped the last encounter, and now they had to trek deeper into the heart of danger? He wasn't sure how much more of this he could take, how much longer he could outrun something that seemed inevitable. But there was no choice. His life wasn't his own anymore.

Evelyn stepped closer, her voice lowering to a whisper meant only for Daniel. "We'll figure this out. I'll help you understand, but for now, we have to survive."

Daniel swallowed hard, nodding even though fear clawed at his insides. The weight of the unknown was crushing him, but Evelyn's words gave him something to hold onto, however fragile it was. The three of them gathered their belongings quickly, the atmosphere in the cabin shifting from uneasy tension to hurried preparation. Marcus double-checked the locks on the doors and windows, while Evelyn packed whatever supplies they could carry. The air felt heavy, thick with the weight of what was coming next. As they stepped outside into the cold night once more, Daniel looked back at the small cabin. It felt like a relic of safety that had already slipped through their fingers. Ahead of them lay more uncertainty, more danger. The sky was overcast now, the moon barely visible through the swirling clouds, casting long shadows on the forest floor. The woods loomed around them, dark and silent, and as they started walking again, Daniel couldn't help but feel that they were heading straight into a trap. A sharp rustling sound came from the trees behind them, followed by a faint voice that carried through the night. It was close. Too close.

Chapter 10: Into the Unknown

The rustling sound in the trees behind them grew louder, sending a shock of fear down Daniel's spine. Marcus stopped dead in his tracks, his hand tightening around the grip of his gun, while Evelyn's head snapped toward the direction of the noise, her eyes narrowing. For a long, tense moment, the three of them stood still, listening to the sounds of the forest. The wind stirred the branches, the leaves rustling softly in the darkness, but beyond that, the woods were eerily quiet. Too quiet.

"We can't keep doing this," Daniel whispered, his voice barely audible, but it carried all the weight of his exhaustion. He was tired of running, tired of the constant fear gnawing at him, but most of all, tired of not knowing why they were being hunted like animals.

Evelyn shot him a sharp glance, her voice barely above a murmur. "We don't have a choice. If we stop, they'll find us."

Marcus motioned for them to move again, leading the way with cautious, measured steps. His every movement was purposeful, quiet, as if even the crunch of a stray leaf underfoot could give away their position. Daniel followed, but his mind raced. The woods felt like a maze of shadows, and every step deeper into it felt like walking into a trap he couldn't escape. The night air was cold against his skin, the scent of pine heavy in the air, mingled with the earthiness of wet soil. Their footsteps were the only sound, the silence pressing down on them like a weight.

"Where are we going, exactly?" Daniel asked, his voice breaking the oppressive quiet.

Evelyn's eyes stayed fixed ahead, but her voice was soft when she answered. "There's an old outpost further up the mountain. It was abandoned decades ago, but it's still secure—if we can get there."

"If?" Daniel's unease only deepened.

"The Order's reach is long," Marcus said without looking back. "But the higher we go, the harder it is for them to operate in the open. Too many eyes in this region. People might ask questions."

Daniel swallowed hard. He wasn't sure he believed that anymore. The Order seemed capable of moving in the shadows, of influencing events without anyone noticing. Who was to say they didn't control the entire region already? Still, it was clear that their only option was to keep moving, and he had to trust that Marcus and Evelyn knew more about this than he did. The further they went into the woods, the more isolated Daniel felt. He'd grown up thinking his life was ordinary—mundane, even—but now every step away from the world he once knew felt like a plunge into something darker, something ancient and deadly.

"Have you ever seen them?" Daniel asked, unable to stop the question. "The people from the Order?"

Evelyn glanced at him. "Once."

Daniel felt a shiver crawl up his spine. "What happened?"

She hesitated, clearly uncomfortable with revisiting whatever memory she was about to share. "It was years ago, during one of the first operations I was a part of. We had intel on a small group of Order operatives who were working out of an estate in the countryside. Our job was to intercept and gather information. But when we got there, it was... too late."

Daniel swallowed. "Too late for what?"

"They were already gone," Evelyn said, her voice tight with the memory. "But what they left behind... let's just say it was enough to show us what they're capable of. They don't leave loose ends."

"What did they leave behind?" Daniel asked, his heart pounding in his chest.

Evelyn's eyes darkened, and for a moment, she looked as though she might not answer. But then, her voice dropped to a whisper. "Bodies. Rituals. Symbols carved into the walls—some kind of language I didn't recognize. They had been performing something, something dark. Whatever it was, they had already completed it by the time we arrived."

Daniel's skin prickled with fear. The way Evelyn spoke, the look in her eyes—it was clear that whatever she had seen had left a mark on her. He could barely wrap his mind around it. Rituals? Symbols? It sounded like something out of a horror story, but this was real. And now, he was tangled in it, whether he liked it or not.

"They're not just after power," Evelyn continued, her voice now cold and detached. "They're after control. Total control. Over governments, over people, and—most of all—over the old bloodlines."

Daniel's pulse quickened. He had heard about secret societies and conspiracies before, but this... this was something else. The Order wasn't just a group of shadowy figures pulling strings from behind the scenes. They were something darker, more dangerous, and they wanted him for a reason that had been buried in centuries of secrets.

"And you?" Daniel asked, glancing at her. "Why are you fighting them?"

Evelyn was silent for a long time. The only sound was the crunch of their footsteps on the forest floor, the rustling of leaves overhead. When she finally spoke, her voice was quiet, almost haunted. "I lost someone to them. Someone important."

Marcus glanced at her, but he didn't say anything. He didn't need to. Daniel could feel the weight of the silence between them. There was a story there, a deep scar that Evelyn wasn't ready to share. He didn't push. Not now. The three of them continued walking, the forest growing denser around them, the air cooler. The trees closed in, their branches stretching like skeletal arms overhead, and Daniel's sense of foreboding only deepened. They were heading into something far worse than he could have imagined. Hours passed, or maybe just minutes—it was hard to tell in the endless stretch of trees. The moonlight was faint now, struggling to break through the thick canopy of leaves, casting strange shadows on the forest floor. Every now and then, Daniel would catch movement out of the corner of his eye—a flicker of something just beyond his sight. But when he turned, there was nothing.

Am I seeing things? he wondered, his nerves raw from fear and exhaustion. But he couldn't shake the feeling that something—or someone—was following them.

Suddenly, Marcus stopped. His hand shot up, signaling for them to freeze. Daniel's heart skipped a beat as he stood still, listening.

"What is it?" Evelyn whispered, her voice barely audible.

Marcus didn't answer at first. He was focused, his eyes scanning the darkness ahead. Then, slowly, he pointed to the trees in the distance. "There," he murmured. "Do you see it?"

Daniel squinted, peering through the shadows. For a moment, he didn't see anything. Just trees and more trees. But then, as his eyes adjusted, he saw it—a faint flicker of movement, something small and fast darting between the trunks.

Evelyn's face tightened. "It's them."

The words sent a bolt of fear through Daniel's chest. "What do we do?"

Marcus's jaw clenched. "We need to move. Now."

Without another word, they started running, their footsteps pounding against the forest floor. Daniel's heart raced, his breath coming in quick, shallow bursts as they weaved between the trees, the sound of movement behind them growing louder.

"They're gaining on us," Evelyn hissed, her voice laced with urgency.

Daniel's lungs burned, his legs aching from the sudden burst of speed. But he couldn't stop. They were close—too close. He could feel it in the air, a cold, unnatural presence that seemed to press down on him from all sides.

"Up ahead!" Marcus called, his voice barely audible over the sound of their feet slamming against the ground.

Daniel's eyes flicked forward, and through the trees, he saw it—a structure, small and half-hidden by the overgrowth. It looked ancient, crumbling, but still standing. It was the outpost Evelyn had mentioned. They reached it just as the first flicker of movement came from behind them—a shadow darting through the trees, closing in fast.

"Inside, now!" Marcus shouted, his voice sharp.

They scrambled through the door, slamming it shut behind them. Marcus immediately set to work, barricading it with anything he could find—old furniture, broken wood—while Evelyn moved to the windows, pulling the heavy shutters closed. Daniel leaned against the wall, his chest heaving as he tried to catch his breath. His mind was spinning, the fear so thick he could barely think. The outpost was dark, the only light coming from the faint glow of the moon seeping through the cracks in the walls.

"What do we do now?" he gasped.

"We hold our ground," Marcus said, his voice hard. "They won't stop until they've found us."

Evelyn's face was set in a grim line. "We don't have much time."

Outside, the woods were silent again, but Daniel knew better. They were out there. Watching. Waiting. Suddenly, the air inside the outpost grew colder, and Daniel felt a chill creep down his spine. A faint, almost imperceptible sound reached his ears—a whisper, soft and haunting, coming from the darkness.

"Did you hear that?" he whispered, his voice shaking.

Evelyn nodded, her face pale. "They're here."

The whispers grew louder, circling the small outpost like a predator closing in on its prey.

Chapter 11: The Haunting Within

The whispers grew louder, a cacophony of hushed voices that seemed to echo off the walls of the old outpost. Daniel's heart raced, every instinct screaming at him to run, but there was nowhere to go. The air was thick with dread, suffocating him as he strained to listen.

"What are they saying?" he whispered, glancing at Evelyn, who was crouched by the window, her expression tense and focused.

"I can't tell," she murmured, her brows furrowing. "It's not in any language I know."

Marcus, still barricading the door, paused for a moment. "It doesn't matter what they're saying. What matters is that they're close."

Daniel's throat tightened, the reality of their situation crashing down on him. "We're trapped," he said, a cold dread seeping into his bones. "They'll break through."

"No," Marcus replied, his voice steady, almost reassuring despite the chaos surrounding them. "This place is built to withstand a siege. If we can hold them off until dawn, we might have a chance."

"A chance?" Daniel echoed, frustration bubbling up inside him. "We're sitting ducks in here! They could be planning their next move right now!"

Evelyn turned her gaze to him, her eyes sharp. "We have to stay calm. Panicking won't help us. We need to think strategically."

Just as she spoke, a heavy thud reverberated through the cabin, shaking the walls and sending dust cascading from the rafters. Daniel's heart dropped as he felt the tremor beneath his feet.

"What was that?" he asked, panic creeping into his voice.

"Sounded like they're testing the door," Marcus said, gritting his teeth as he shoved another piece of furniture against it. "We need to prepare ourselves."

Evelyn stood, moving closer to Daniel. "Listen to me, Daniel. If they breach the door, we have to stick together. We can't let them divide us."

"I know," he replied, but his voice was barely above a whisper. The weight of the situation pressed down on him, making it hard to breathe. "But what if they come after me? What if I'm the target?"

"You're not just a target. You're the key," Evelyn said, her eyes fierce. "That's why they'll do everything to capture you. But you can't let fear control you. You have to fight."

The determination in her voice resonated with him, igniting a flicker of courage. Daniel nodded, clenching his fists. "I'll fight," he vowed, though the truth was that he didn't even know how.

The whispers outside turned into a low chant, an unsettling rhythm that throbbed through the air. Daniel felt it in his bones—a primal fear that clawed at his sanity. He could almost make out words—phrases that twisted like shadows in his mind, echoing the horror of Evelyn's earlier account. A sudden crash echoed from the door, and Daniel stumbled back, his heart racing. Marcus braced himself against the wood, sweat glistening on his brow. "They're trying to break in. Get ready!"

Evelyn pulled out her knife, gripping it tightly as she stood by the window, her eyes scanning the darkness outside. "We need to know how many there are," she said urgently. "If we can see them..."

Daniel nodded and moved to her side, peering through the grimy glass. The darkness outside was nearly impenetrable, but through the shadows, he could see vague figures moving, their forms blurred like ghosts. The whispers intensified, a haunting symphony that seemed to seep into his mind.

"God, there are so many," Daniel breathed, his voice barely a whisper. He felt the blood drain from his face as he tried to count the shapes, but they moved too swiftly, like phantoms dancing just beyond his reach.

"They're surrounding us," Evelyn said, her tone grim. "We need to find another way out."

"There's a cellar," Marcus interjected, breathing heavily as he steadied himself against the door. "It leads deeper into the mountain. If we can make it down there, we might lose them."

"Let's do it," Daniel urged, determination coursing through him now, the adrenaline kicking in. "We can't stay here."

Marcus moved quickly, leading the way toward the back of the cabin. The sound of wood splintering filled the air as the door began to crack under the relentless pressure. Daniel's heart raced faster than ever as he followed Marcus and Evelyn down a narrow staircase that led into darkness. The cellar was damp and musty, the air heavy with the scent of earth. The dim light from a small window high above barely illuminated the stone walls, casting long shadows that seemed to dance ominously.

"Close the door," Marcus ordered, urgency in his voice. They quickly shut the heavy wooden door behind them, sealing them off from the chaos above.

Daniel pressed his ear against the door, straining to listen. The sound of shouts filtered down to them, the cacophony of a struggle mingling with the whispers. It sent chills racing down his spine.

"They're in," he whispered, the reality crashing over him like a wave. "What do we do now?"

Evelyn pulled out a flashlight, its beam cutting through the darkness. "We find a way out," she said, determination etched on her face. "This place must have an escape route."

As they moved deeper into the cellar, the air felt cooler, almost alive with anticipation. Shadows loomed larger as they ventured into the unknown. Daniel's heart pounded louder with every step, each echo a reminder of the danger just outside the door.

"Here," Marcus said, pointing to a wooden door at the far end of the cellar. "Let's check this one."

Daniel's breath caught in his throat as they approached. The door looked old, its edges rough and weathered, as if it hadn't been opened in years. A faint light flickered from beneath it, and a low hum vibrated through the air, sending shivers up his spine.

"What is that?" Daniel asked, glancing at Evelyn.

"Only one way to find out," she replied, her voice steady despite the fear etched across her features.

With a nod, Marcus grasped the handle and turned it, pushing the door open slowly. It creaked ominously, and the smell of musty air hit them like a wall. The room beyond was filled with old crates and barrels, their surfaces coated with dust, but it was the large, intricate markings on the walls that caught Daniel's attention.

"What is this place?" he breathed, stepping inside.

"It looks like a storage room," Evelyn said, shining the flashlight around. "But these symbols... I've seen them before." She moved closer to the walls, tracing her fingers over the carvings. "This is part of the same language as the symbols I saw before—the ones from the estate."

"Are you sure?" Daniel asked, feeling a mix of curiosity and dread.

"Yes," she confirmed, her eyes widening with recognition. "This is significant. We might be onto something important."

Marcus moved toward a crate, prying it open with a crowbar he had found nearby. Inside, he pulled out what appeared to be old books, their spines cracked and worn. "These might contain information about the Order, or even about your family," he said, handing one to Evelyn.

As she took it, Daniel noticed the tremor in her hands. "We need to find a way to decipher these," she said, her voice almost breathless. "They could hold the key to everything."

Just then, the sound of heavy footsteps echoed from the doorway they had just left, the door rattling under the weight of whatever was trying to breach it. Daniel's heart raced, and he glanced at Marcus and Evelyn, fear etched on their faces.

"We need to hurry," Marcus said, his voice urgent. "If they get in here, we're done for."

They rifled through the crates, urgency propelling them. Daniel grabbed a handful of papers, the faded ink barely legible under the flashlight's beam. As he skimmed through the pages, one word caught his eye—Ascendant.

"Wait," he said, the word sparking something within him. "What does this mean? What's an Ascendant?"

Evelyn's eyes widened as she read over his shoulder. "It's mentioned in the context of the bloodline. It's a title... a role. The Ascendant is someone who possesses the key to unlocking the power of their lineage."

Daniel's breath caught in his throat. "And that's me, isn't it?"

"Yes," Evelyn said, her voice a mix of awe and fear. "You are the last of your line, Daniel. If the Order realizes that, they'll stop at nothing to take you."

A loud crash shook the room, and the door splintered under the pressure. Daniel's heart raced as he quickly shoved the papers into his backpack, adrenaline surging through him.

"We have to get out of here," Marcus said, urgency flashing in his eyes. "Now!"

Evelyn nodded, her expression fierce. "There has to be another exit."

They quickly scanned the room, searching for any way out as the door buckled under the relentless force outside. Panic gripped Daniel, but he forced himself to focus. They couldn't get trapped here—not now.

"Over there!" he shouted, pointing to a narrow passage hidden behind a stack of crates.

Marcus grabbed a nearby crate and pushed it aside, revealing the dark opening. "Let's go!" he urged, leading the way as they slipped into the tunnel. The space was tight, the walls rough against their skin, but they moved quickly, driven by the urgency of their escape. The sound of the door finally giving way echoed behind them, a reminder of the danger pursuing them.

"Keep moving!" Marcus called, his voice a steady anchor in the chaos.

As they plunged deeper into the darkness, Daniel's mind raced. The words Ascendant echoed in his thoughts, mingling with the fear and uncertainty that consumed him. What did it mean? What power did it hold?

But before he could delve deeper into his thoughts, a loud noise erupted from behind them—shouts mixed with the sounds of footsteps rushing into the cellar.

"Go! Go!" Marcus yelled, pushing them forward.

The passage opened up into a larger chamber, illuminated by flickering torches along the stone walls. It felt ancient, the air heavy with the weight of history, and Daniel caught sight of more symbols etched into the rock.

"Look!" Evelyn exclaimed, rushing forward, her flashlight beam illuminating a massive stone tablet at the far end of the chamber.

Daniel's breath caught in his throat. The tablet was covered in the same markings they had seen earlier. "What does it say?" he asked, moving closer, drawn to its power.

"I don't know," Evelyn said, her eyes wide with wonder. "But it's crucial. If we can decipher it, it might reveal how to stop the Order."

Before they could study it further, another crash reverberated through the tunnel, followed by the unmistakable sound of heavy footsteps.

"They're coming!" Marcus shouted, his voice laced with urgency. "We need to move—now!"

With a final glance at the tablet, Daniel felt a mix of fear and determination. They were running out of time, and he was beginning to understand the gravity of the path laid out before him. The answers lay within the depths of this ancient world, but the Order was hot on their trail, ready to extinguish the last flickers of hope.

"Let's go!" he urged, leading the way deeper into the shadows as the sounds of pursuit grew louder, echoing off the stone walls.

As they raced through the chamber, Daniel couldn't shake the feeling that every step they took was leading them further into a trap. But with the weight of destiny resting on his shoulders, he knew he had no choice. The past was calling, and he was ready to answer.

Chapter 12: The Veil of Secrets

The air grew colder as they pressed deeper into the winding passage, the flickering torches casting erratic shadows that danced along the walls. Daniel felt a gnawing anxiety in his gut, the weight of what lay ahead pressing heavily on his mind. He stole a glance at Marcus and Evelyn, who moved with purpose, their determination radiating despite the looming danger.

"Where does this lead?" Daniel asked, trying to keep his voice steady, though his heart thundered in his chest.

"Not sure," Marcus replied, glancing back. "But it feels like we're in some sort of ancient hideout. We need to find an exit before they catch up with us."

As they navigated the narrow path, Daniel's mind raced with questions. The stone tablet, the symbols—it all felt connected to his family, to the power he might wield as the Ascendant. But the more he thought about it, the more overwhelming it became. He felt the weight of expectation on his shoulders, pressing down like a physical burden.

"We have to find a way to decipher those symbols," Evelyn said, her voice breaking through his thoughts. "They could provide crucial information about your lineage and the Order."

Daniel nodded, but uncertainty gnawed at him. "What if it reveals something we're not ready for? What if it shows that I'm not the hero in this story?"

Evelyn turned to him, her eyes fierce. "You are not alone in this. We're in this together, and we'll figure it out. Just trust us."

"Trust," he repeated, the word feeling heavy in his mouth. He had spent so long feeling like an outsider, even within his own family.

Could he truly embrace this new reality, this role that had been thrust upon him?

As they continued down the darkened corridor, they stumbled upon another chamber, this one larger and adorned with intricate carvings. The light from the torches illuminated scenes of battles long forgotten, figures cloaked in shadows engaged in fierce combat against a backdrop of swirling mist.

"Look at this," Marcus breathed, his eyes wide with awe. "It's like a mural of history."

Daniel stepped closer, tracing the carvings with his fingers. Each image told a story, a narrative of conflict and struggle. He could almost feel the weight of those who had come before him, their spirits lingering in the air.

"What if this place is a sanctuary?" Evelyn suggested, her voice barely above a whisper. "A place where the last remnants of your family sought refuge from the Order."

"Sanctuary or tomb," Daniel muttered, a shiver running down his spine. "It could be both."

Suddenly, a loud crash echoed from the direction they had come, jolting him back to reality. Daniel's heart raced as he turned, the urgency of their situation crashing down around him. The Order was relentless, and every moment they spent here put them closer to being captured.

"Come on!" he urged, pushing forward into the chamber. "We can't stay here!"

They moved quickly, scanning the room for any possible exit. The air grew heavier with each passing second, tension crackling like electricity as they searched for a way out. Daniel's instincts kicked in, urging him to keep moving, to push through the fear that threatened to paralyze him.

"Over here!" Marcus called, pointing to a narrow passage that seemed to lead deeper into the bowels of the sanctuary. "It might be our way out."

They dashed toward it, the sounds of pursuit growing ever closer. The adrenaline coursed through Daniel's veins, driving him forward as they entered the new tunnel. The darkness enveloped them, the sound of their footsteps echoing in the confined space.

"Keep your eyes peeled," Marcus instructed, his voice low but steady. "We don't know what's waiting for us."

As they continued down the passage, the walls began to narrow, forcing them closer together. Daniel felt Evelyn's presence beside him, a small comfort amid the chaos. The rhythmic sound of their breathing mixed with the distant shouts of the Order, reminding him of the urgency of their escape.

Then, as they rounded a corner, a glimmer caught Daniel's eye—a faint light spilling from an opening at the end of the tunnel. Hope surged within him as they approached, the light beckoning like a siren's call.

"Is that an exit?" Evelyn asked, her voice tinged with excitement.

"Looks like it," Marcus replied, quickening his pace. "Let's move!"

As they neared the opening, Daniel felt a rush of exhilaration. They could almost taste freedom, the air outside beckoning them like a long-lost friend. But as they reached the light, their hearts sank—what lay beyond was not the open sky they had hoped for. Instead, they emerged into a vast cavern, the ceiling stretching high above them, adorned with sparkling crystals that cast ethereal patterns across the stone walls. The ground was uneven, littered with rocks and debris, and in the center of the cavern stood a massive stone pedestal.

"What is this place?" Daniel wondered aloud, taking a cautious step forward.

"It looks like a ceremonial site," Evelyn replied, her voice filled with awe. "The pedestal... it might have held something significant."

Daniel approached the pedestal, the smooth surface glinting under the crystal light. Carvings adorned its sides, much like the ones in the previous chamber, but these were different—more intricate, more profound. They spoke of ancient rites and secrets long forgotten.

"This is it," Daniel said, a sense of realization dawning upon him. "This is connected to my family. I can feel it."

Before he could delve deeper into his thoughts, a loud rumble echoed through the cavern, followed by a shower of dust cascading from the ceiling. The ground trembled beneath them, and panic surged in Daniel's chest.

"We need to go, now!" Marcus shouted, urgency coloring his voice.

But as they turned to retreat, they were met with a chilling sight. Figures emerged from the shadows, their silhouettes illuminated by the light of the cavern. Clad in dark robes, the members of the Order advanced toward them, their eyes glinting with a sinister determination.

"Trapped like rats," one of them sneered, stepping forward, revealing a face that was both familiar and terrifying. "You should have known better than to come here, Daniel."

"Damon," Daniel breathed, recognition flooding his senses. The betrayal twisted in his gut like a knife.

"Surprised to see me?" Damon chuckled, the sound echoing ominously. "You thought you could escape our grasp? You were wrong."

Daniel felt a surge of anger, a fire igniting within him. "What do you want from me?"

Damon stepped closer, his voice low and menacing. "You are the Ascendant. You possess the key to everything we seek. Hand it over, and perhaps I'll consider letting you live."

"No!" Evelyn shouted, stepping protectively in front of Daniel. "We won't let you take him!"

The members of the Order laughed, their voices chilling. "You think you can protect him? You're outnumbered and outmatched."

As they closed in, Daniel's heart raced, the realization crashing down on him. They were surrounded, the walls closing in. Panic threatened to overwhelm him, but beneath it all, a flicker of defiance ignited.

"No!" he shouted, stepping forward. "You don't understand what you're dealing with!"

Damon's eyes narrowed. "What are you talking about?"

The air around Daniel crackled with energy, and for the first time, he felt a strange power surging within him. It coursed through his veins, igniting something deep inside—an ancestral connection that called to him.

"I am not just a pawn in your game," he declared, his voice steady and unwavering. "I am the Ascendant, and you will not take me."

A tense silence fell over the cavern as the members of the Order shifted, uncertainty flashing across their faces. But before they could react, Daniel felt the energy reach its peak, a surge of light bursting forth from him.

"Run!" he shouted to Marcus and Evelyn as he unleashed the energy, the force of it pushing against the Order, sending them reeling backward.

The explosion of light illuminated the cavern, casting the shadows away momentarily. Daniel's heart raced as he turned to flee, his friends right behind him. They dashed through the cavern, the sounds of chaos fading behind them as they navigated back into the tunnels. As they raced away, adrenaline fueled their escape. Daniel's mind spun with the implications of what had just happened. He had tapped into something powerful, a strength he never knew he possessed. But with that power came a greater danger—a target on his back that would only grow larger.

"Keep going!" Marcus urged, leading the way through the dark passage. "We have to put as much distance between us and them as possible!"

Breathless and desperate, they navigated the labyrinth of tunnels, urgency driving them forward. But deep down, Daniel knew that this was only the beginning. The Order would not give up easily, and with the revelations of his lineage, he had awakened a storm that would change everything. As they emerged into the cool night air, the stars twinkling above them like distant beacons, Daniel felt a mix of exhilaration and dread. The fight was far from over, and the path ahead was fraught with peril.

"We need to regroup and figure out our next move," Evelyn said, her voice steady despite the fear in her eyes.

Daniel nodded, determination flooding his veins. "And I need to understand what

it means to be the Ascendant. If we're going to defeat the Order, I have to learn how to wield this power."

Together, they stood on the precipice of a new chapter in their lives, the night stretching before them like an uncharted sea. The challenges ahead would test their resolve, but united, they would face whatever darkness lay ahead. As Daniel looked to his friends, he felt a flicker of hope ignite within him—a hope that whispered of victory, of reclaiming what was lost, and of uncovering the truth buried deep within the shadows.

Chapter 14: Echoes of the Past

The night air was crisp, carrying with it a palpable sense of foreboding as Daniel, Marcus, and Evelyn regrouped in a secluded clearing surrounded by dense trees. The moon hung low in the sky, casting an ethereal glow that illuminated their faces, revealing the exhaustion etched in their features.

"We need to find somewhere safe," Marcus suggested, glancing nervously over his shoulder. "They'll be searching for us."

Daniel nodded, his heart still racing from the encounter in the cavern. "There's an old abandoned cabin a few miles from here. It might be the perfect place to lay low and figure out our next steps."

Evelyn studied him, concern flashing in her eyes. "Are you sure it's safe? The Order won't stop until they find you, and they have resources we can't even begin to imagine."

"We'll have to take that risk," Daniel replied, a sense of resolve building within him. "I can't run forever. I need to understand who I am and what it means to be the Ascendant. The only way to do that is to confront this head-on."

As they moved, the silence of the forest enveloped them, broken only by the sound of their footsteps on the leaf-strewn ground. Daniel's mind churned with thoughts, wrestling with the revelations that had unfolded before him. He had tapped into a power that had been dormant within him, yet he was still largely ignorant of what it truly meant.

"Do you think what happened back there was just a fluke?" Evelyn asked, her voice breaking the quiet.

"No," Daniel said firmly. "It felt real—like something awakened inside of me. I can't explain it, but I know there's more to uncover."

"Maybe we can find some sort of guide," Marcus suggested. "Someone who understands the Ascendant and can help you harness that power."

"Like who?" Daniel countered, frustration creeping into his voice. "Everyone I've known has been in the dark about this. I'm not sure where to start."

Evelyn fell silent, her brow furrowed as she contemplated their situation. "There might be records—old texts or documents that talk about the Ascendant. If we can find them, it could lead us to someone who knows what we're up against."

The idea sparked a glimmer of hope in Daniel's chest. "The family estate," he said suddenly, recalling the vast library he had visited only a handful of times in his life. "There could be something there—books, journals, anything related to our family's history."

"Then that's where we'll go," Marcus declared, determination lacing his words. "But first, let's get to that cabin. We can regroup and plan from there."

They quickened their pace, weaving through the trees until they finally reached the dilapidated cabin. Its once vibrant exterior had faded over the years, but it still stood defiantly against the encroaching wilderness. Daniel felt a sense of nostalgia wash over him as he pushed the creaking door open, the hinges protesting against the intrusion. Inside, dust motes floated lazily in the dim light, the air thick with the scent of aged wood and decay. A shiver ran down Daniel's spine, but he quickly dismissed it; this place held memories of his childhood—a place where he had felt safe before life had turned upside down.

"Let's barricade the door," Marcus suggested, moving towards a nearby shelf. "We need to make sure we're secure."

As they worked together to fortify the cabin, Daniel's mind drifted back to the power he had felt in the cavern. He couldn't shake the thought that it was somehow linked to his family's past.

"What if," he began slowly, "the power of the Ascendant is tied to the legacy of my family? What if the key to unlocking it lies in the history that we've forgotten?"

Evelyn stopped her movements and turned to face him. "What do you mean?"

"I've seen the carvings and symbols; they allude to ancient knowledge, rituals that my ancestors might have practiced. If we can uncover that history, maybe we can figure out how to control what I experienced."

Marcus paused, his eyes narrowing in thought. "You could be right. If the Order is after you for your power, it stands to reason that they'd want to extinguish any connection you have to it."

Daniel felt a rush of determination surge through him. "Then it's settled. We'll sift through whatever we can find in the family estate. I won't let them dictate my fate."

With the cabin secured, they gathered in the dimly lit room, the flickering light from a small lantern casting long shadows on the walls. Daniel felt a surge of gratitude for his friends—this journey would be impossible without their support.

"What's our plan?" Marcus asked, breaking the silence that had settled over them.

"We'll wait until dawn, then head to the estate," Daniel replied. "We'll need to move quickly and quietly. If the Order is still tracking us, they won't take long to figure out where we are."

The three of them spent the rest of the night in uneasy silence, taking turns keeping watch while the others rested. Daniel couldn't shake the feeling of being watched, a chill creeping up his spine as shadows danced along the walls. As dawn broke, a soft light seeped through the cracks in the cabin walls, bathing the room in a warm glow. Daniel's eyes fluttered open, his mind still heavy with fatigue but invigorated by purpose.

"Time to move," he said, his voice steady. They gathered their things and prepared for the journey ahead, adrenaline coursing through their veins.

As they stepped outside, the forest was alive with the sounds of morning—birds chirping, leaves rustling in the gentle breeze. But Daniel couldn't shake the feeling of impending danger that loomed over them like a storm cloud.

"Let's stick together," Marcus advised, his eyes scanning the surroundings. "We'll take the back roads to avoid drawing attention."

The three of them moved through the forest, the path winding and treacherous. Daniel led the way, determined to reach the estate as quickly as possible. Each step felt like a step closer to uncovering the truth, yet also felt laden with the weight of what they might discover. Hours passed as they navigated the dense underbrush, finally emerging onto the overgrown path that led to the family estate. The mansion stood before them, majestic yet forlorn, its grandeur diminished by years of neglect. Daniel's heart raced as he approached, memories flooding back—laughter, warmth, a sense of belonging that had long since faded.

"This place gives me the creeps," Marcus muttered, glancing around as if expecting someone to jump out from the shadows.

"We need to be careful," Evelyn cautioned, her voice low. "The Order could already be watching."

Daniel nodded, the weight of their mission pressing down on him. As they stepped inside, the air was thick with dust and memories. He felt a strange connection to the walls, a sense of familiarity mingled with an overwhelming feeling of loss.

"Where do we start?" Marcus asked, surveying the vast expanse of the room, which was filled with dusty furniture and faded portraits of ancestors long gone.

"Let's check the library first," Daniel suggested, remembering the numerous times he had lost himself in the pages of books as a child. "If there's anything related to the Ascendant, it will likely be there."

They made their way down the grand hallway, the sound of their footsteps echoing off the walls. Daniel felt a mixture of excitement and dread; the answers they sought were here, hidden among the remnants of his family's legacy. As they entered the library, the scent of aged paper enveloped them, and Daniel felt a rush of nostalgia. The room was lined with towering shelves, filled with books that had been untouched for years. Dust danced in the light streaming through the tall windows, illuminating the intricate carvings on the shelves.

"Look at this," Evelyn said, pulling a large leather-bound tome from a shelf. The title was worn, but Daniel could make out the words Legends of the Ascendant.

His heart raced as he reached for it, the weight of the book heavy in his hands. "This could be it," he murmured, flipping it open to reveal pages filled with ancient script and illustrations of the Ascendant throughout history.

"Can you read it?" Marcus asked, leaning closer to see.

"Some of it," Daniel replied, his eyes scanning the text. "It's written in an old dialect, but I think I can decipher it."

As he read aloud, the words began to weave a tapestry of knowledge—a history of the Ascendant, their powers, their struggles against the Order, and the sacrifices made to protect the realm from darkness.

"Listen to this," Daniel said, excitement lacing his voice. "The Ascendant is said to possess a unique connection to the past, able to draw upon the strength of their ancestors. It's a power that can be harnessed but also feared, as it attracts those who seek to control it."

Evelyn's eyes widened. "That explains why the Order is after you. They want to exploit that power."

"Exactly," Daniel said, a sense of urgency building within him. "But there's more—according to this, to fully awaken the Ascendant's power, a specific ritual must be performed. It involves gathering the three sacred relics of my family."

"What relics?" Marcus asked, curiosity piquing.

"An ancient dagger, a pendant, and a scroll—the keys to unlocking my potential," Daniel explained, feeling a newfound sense of purpose

"But where do we find them?" Evelyn asked, glancing at the stacks of books that loomed over them like watchful guardians.

"The book suggests they were hidden throughout our ancestral lands," Daniel replied, flipping through the pages until he found a rough map. "If we can find the locations, we might uncover the relics before the Order can catch up to us."

As he traced the path on the map, a sudden noise echoed from outside the library—footsteps. The sound grew louder, accompanied by the unmistakable murmur of voices.

"They're here," Marcus hissed, panic rising in his voice. "We need to hide!"

Daniel's heart raced as they quickly scrambled to find a place to conceal themselves. He could feel the pressure of time closing in, the weight of his destiny pressing down on him.

"Quick, behind the shelves!" Evelyn whispered urgently, pushing Daniel into a narrow space just as the library door swung open.

They held their breath as dark figures entered the room, their silhouettes sharp against the fading light. Daniel's pulse thundered in his ears, the reality of their situation sinking in.

"Search everywhere," one of the figures commanded, their voice laced with authority. "The Ascendant is here. We need to find him before he uncovers the truth."

Daniel exchanged a frantic glance with Marcus and Evelyn. This was it—this was the moment that would define everything. They had to escape and complete the ritual to harness his power before the Order could stop them. As the figures moved closer, Daniel felt the weight of the book in his hand, the knowledge it contained a beacon of hope. The answers lay within the pages, and he would do everything in his power to unlock his destiny.

Just then, a loud crash echoed from outside the library, the sound of shattering glass punctuating the tension in the air.

"Check the back entrance!" a voice shouted.

Daniel's heart dropped as he realized the Order was closing in on them, and the hidden paths were now compromised. He could almost hear the sound of his own heartbeat, pounding in his ears like a war drum.

"This is it," he whispered to Evelyn and Marcus, fear flooding his chest. "We need to make a choice—stay hidden and hope for the best, or make a run for it and risk everything."

The decision loomed over them, heavier than ever, as the shadows grew closer, surrounding them with uncertainty.

"Daniel," Marcus urged, desperation creeping into his voice. "What do we do?"

Before Daniel could respond, the door creaked ominously as it began to swing open, revealing the dark figures beyond. The light from the hallway silhouetted their faces, and he knew—this was the moment that would define everything. With no time left, he inhaled deeply, adrenaline surging through him, and made the decision that would change the course of their destiny forever.

Chapter 15: The Breaking Point

Daniel's breath caught in his throat as the door creaked open, the dark silhouettes of the Order's agents looming just beyond the threshold. Time seemed to slow, every second feeling like an eternity as his heart thundered in his chest. He glanced at Evelyn and Marcus, both of them frozen in place, their eyes wide with fear.

"Daniel, now!" Evelyn's voice was barely more than a whisper, but it carried the weight of urgency that pierced through the fog of terror clouding his mind.

Without thinking, Daniel surged forward. His body moved on instinct, his feet pounding against the creaky floorboards as he bolted toward the far end of the library. Evelyn and Marcus were right behind him, their rapid footsteps blending with the commotion of the Order's agents flooding into the room.

"After them!" a voice barked from behind, echoing through the library like a death sentence.

They sprinted through the rows of dusty bookshelves, weaving between the towering stacks that seemed to close in around them, creating a maze of shadows. Daniel's mind raced as fast as his legs, trying to formulate a plan, a way out—anything.

"This way!" he hissed, yanking a narrow door open that led into a service passage. The scent of damp stone and mildew wafted out, a stark contrast to the dusty, stale air of the library. They slipped through just as the agents rounded the corner, slamming the door behind them with a deafening thud.

The hallway was narrow, claustrophobic, and the only light came from a faint, flickering bulb dangling from the ceiling like a forgotten remnant of another time. The walls felt like they were closing in, pressing on Daniel's shoulders as they hurried forward, their breathing ragged in the oppressive silence.

"They're too close," Marcus panted, glancing over his shoulder. "We're not going to make it!"

"Yes, we will," Daniel replied, his voice firm though his chest was tight with fear. "Just keep moving."

The tunnel twisted and turned, leading deeper into the labyrinthine bowels of the mansion. It seemed endless, each corner revealing more darkness. The sound of the Order's footsteps behind them echoed through the tight space, growing louder with each passing moment.

"How far does this thing go?" Marcus muttered under his breath.

"Far enough, I hope," Daniel said, though doubt gnawed at him. They had to reach the back entrance—the only other exit from the mansion besides the main gates. But it was a gamble. If the Order had already anticipated their route, they were heading straight into a trap.

They burst through another door at the end of the tunnel, emerging into a small, windowless room lit only by a weak beam of light filtering through cracks in the ceiling. Old crates and forgotten relics cluttered the space, remnants of lives long gone.

Evelyn immediately slammed the door shut behind them, her fingers trembling as she fumbled to latch the lock. "That'll slow them down," she muttered, though her voice carried no conviction.

Daniel crossed the room to a trapdoor in the corner, his fingers searching for the rusted iron ring that would pull it open. The moment his hands closed around it, he yanked with all his strength, the wood groaning as the door finally gave way with a loud creak.

Below was a narrow stone stairwell, descending into an inky black void. The air that rose from it was cold and damp, like breathing in the very essence of the earth itself.

"Down there?" Marcus asked, his face pale as he peered into the darkness.

"It's the only way," Daniel said, swallowing the unease that curled in his stomach. "The passage should lead outside the estate grounds."

"Should?" Evelyn raised an eyebrow, though there was no time for argument. The sound of footsteps and muffled voices behind the door was growing louder.

"Let's go," Daniel urged, already lowering himself into the stairwell. One by one, they followed, descending into the pitch black as the door above them rattled violently.

As they went deeper into the stone passageway, the darkness swallowed them entirely. There were no lights here—only the sound of their breathing and the rhythmic drip of water echoing through the cavernous space. The walls were damp to the touch, and every step down felt like they were descending further into the heart of the unknown.

Evelyn's hand brushed against Daniel's arm in the darkness. "How much further?" she whispered.

"We're close," Daniel said, though he wasn't entirely sure. The last time he'd been down here was as a child, running through the tunnels with his cousins. The memory was foggy at best, but he prayed the exit was still there, still functional.

The narrow stairwell finally opened into a larger chamber, the ceiling rising high above them. Daniel fumbled for the lantern he had brought with him from the mansion, quickly striking a match to ignite the wick. A dim light flickered to life, revealing the expanse of the underground chamber. The room was ancient, its stone walls carved with symbols Daniel recognized from the Ascendant texts they had found earlier. His heart skipped a beat as he realized where they were.

"This isn't just a passage," he murmured, his eyes scanning the intricate carvings. "It's a sanctuary."

Evelyn moved closer to one of the walls, her fingers lightly tracing the ancient symbols. "What is this place?"

Daniel knelt by an altar in the center of the room, where an ornate box rested—its surface etched with the same markings as the walls. His hand hovered over it, a strange pull tugging at him, compelling him to open it.

"This..." Daniel's voice was soft, almost reverent. "This is what they've been looking for."

He lifted the lid of the box, revealing a small, gleaming pendant. The moment his fingers touched it, a surge of energy shot through him, unlike anything he had ever felt before. His vision blurred, his mind overwhelmed by a flood of images—ancient battles, rituals, faces of long-forgotten ancestors.

The power of the Ascendant.

"Daniel?" Evelyn's voice broke through the haze, grounding him. He looked up at her, his breath shallow, his hand still clutching the pendant.

"They're here," Marcus whispered urgently from the far end of the room, his voice tight with fear. He gestured toward the passage they had come through—the sound of the Order's agents was unmistakable now, their footsteps echoing in the stairwell.

Daniel's grip on the pendant tightened. He could feel the power coursing through him, stronger than before. The ritual was incomplete, but the relics were here—within his reach. If they could hold off the Order just a little longer...

"Do we fight or run?" Marcus asked, his eyes darting between Daniel and the passage.

"We don't have time to run," Daniel replied, standing. He felt different now—stronger, more focused. The pendant pulsed in his hand, its power intertwining with his own. "We fight."

Evelyn stepped beside him, her eyes steady and determined. "Then let's give them hell."

The door at the far end of the chamber burst open, and the dark figures of the Order swarmed in. Daniel stood his ground, the pendant glowing faintly in his hand. The energy within him surged, and he could feel it building, waiting to be unleashed.

"Daniel!" Evelyn shouted, but the sound was drowned out by the rush of power as it exploded from him. The chamber filled with blinding light, and for a moment, everything was silent, still.

When the light faded, Daniel stood alone in the center of the room. The agents were gone, their forms reduced to shadows on the walls. He staggered, his body weak from the effort, but the power still hummed within him, barely contained.

"Daniel..." Marcus breathed, his voice filled with awe. "What did you just do?"

Daniel swayed on his feet, his vision blurring as exhaustion took hold. He tried to answer, but the words wouldn't come. Then, everything went black.

Chapter 16: Beneath the Ashes

Daniel woke to darkness. The world around him was silent, except for the faint sound of his own breathing. He blinked several times, but the blackness remained absolute, suffocating in its depth. For a moment, he wasn't sure if his eyes were open at all. His head throbbed, the remnants of the power surge pulsing through him like an aftershock.

"Daniel?" Evelyn's voice cut through the haze, faint but present. His heart lurched at the sound of it, and he turned his head in her direction.

"I'm here," he croaked, his voice hoarse. His throat felt raw, as though he hadn't spoken in hours, and every word scratched at his dry mouth.

Slowly, the details of the chamber around him began to emerge—faint outlines in the shadows, stone walls looming overhead, the altar still standing in the center of the room. The pendant hung from his neck now, its weight against his chest a constant reminder of the immense power it held.

"How long was I out?" he asked, struggling to sit up. His muscles ached, his limbs sluggish as if his body had been drained of all energy.

"Not long," Marcus replied, his voice strained. Daniel glanced toward him and noticed Marcus leaning heavily against the far wall, a makeshift bandage wrapped around his arm. Blood had soaked through the cloth, but Marcus seemed to be holding it together. Barely.

"The Order?" Daniel asked, trying to push through the fog that still clouded his mind.

"They're gone," Evelyn answered, her voice low. She was crouched near Marcus, examining his wound. "At least, the ones who were down here. You—" she paused, looking over at Daniel with something that resembled both awe and fear, "you did something, and they just... vanished."

Daniel's brow furrowed. He tried to recall those final moments, the rush of energy that had surged through him, but the memory was fractured, like looking at broken shards of glass. He remembered the light, the power exploding outward, but everything after that was a blur.

"I didn't mean to—" he began, but Evelyn shook her head.

"You saved us," she said softly, her hand resting on Marcus's shoulder. "We would've been dead if you hadn't stopped them."

Daniel let out a shaky breath, the weight of what he had done settling over him. The power of the Ascendant was unlike anything he had imagined, far more potent than the texts had suggested. And now, that power was his.

But at what cost?

He looked down at the pendant hanging around his neck, its surface glinting faintly even in the low light. It seemed almost dormant now, as though it were waiting for something—for him. The energy that had surged through him felt like it had been only the beginning, a fraction of what the Ascendant was capable of.

"Can you walk?" Evelyn asked, interrupting his thoughts. She stood, brushing the dust from her clothes, and offered him a hand.

Daniel nodded, though his body protested the movement. "I'll manage."

He took her hand and pulled himself to his feet, his legs trembling beneath him as they adjusted to the weight. His head spun, but he steadied himself, inhaling deeply to center his thoughts.

"We need to move," Marcus said, wincing as he shifted his arm. "There's no way the Order will let this go. They'll send more after us once they realize their team is missing."

Daniel knew he was right. The Order wouldn't stop until they had the Ascendant in their grasp—and now that Daniel had bonded with the pendant, they would come for him with renewed ferocity.

"We need to get out of the estate," Daniel said, glancing toward the tunnel they had come through. "There's an exit at the end of this passage, but we'll have to move fast."

They made their way down the stone stairwell, moving cautiously but with a sense of urgency. Daniel's body felt heavy with exhaustion, but he pushed through, his mind focused on what lay ahead. He couldn't shake the feeling that their enemies were already closing in, that every second they spent underground was a second too long. The tunnel stretched on, the stone walls pressing in on them as they descended deeper into the earth. The air grew colder, more stagnant, and the sound of dripping water echoed in the silence. The weight of the pendant against his chest felt heavier now, as though it were pulling him toward something—a destination just out of reach.

"Where exactly does this lead?" Marcus asked, his voice strained as he clutched his injured arm.

"There's an old exit from the estate grounds," Daniel replied, his voice low. "A hidden path that leads into the forest. My ancestors used it during the wars to escape when the estate was under siege."

"Convenient," Marcus muttered.

"Let's hope it's still intact," Daniel said. He wasn't entirely sure. The last time he had been down here, he had barely been old enough to understand what the tunnels were for, much less navigate them.

The passage eventually opened into a larger cavern, the ceiling stretching high above them. At the far end, Daniel could see the faint outline of a wooden door, half-rotted and covered in thick layers of dust. Beyond that door was the forest—freedom.

"We're almost there," he said, quickening his pace.

As they approached the door, a strange sensation washed over Daniel. It was as if the air had shifted, charged with a new kind of energy. He stopped in his tracks, his body going rigid as a sudden, overwhelming sense of dread flooded through him.

"Wait," he said, his voice tight. "Something's wrong."

Evelyn and Marcus froze, their eyes darting toward him. "What is it?" Evelyn asked, her hand instinctively reaching for the dagger she kept strapped to her waist.

"I don't know," Daniel replied, his eyes scanning the cavern. The sensation was growing stronger, pulsing through him like a warning. His hand reached up to grasp the pendant at his chest, and the moment his fingers touched it, he felt the pull again—this time more intense.

Without thinking, Daniel reached out toward the door. But just before his hand made contact, a blinding flash of light erupted from the center of the room, knocking him backward with a force that stole the breath from his lungs. When he hit the ground, his vision swam, and for a moment, he thought he had lost consciousness again. But the light was still there, glowing in the center of the cavern, flickering like a flame.

"What the hell is that?" Marcus whispered, his voice trembling.

Daniel pushed himself up, his eyes locked on the light. It was no ordinary light—it was alive, pulsing with energy that resonated deep within him. It was as if the cavern itself had come to life, responding to the power of the Ascendant.

"We need to leave," Evelyn urged, pulling Daniel to his feet. "Now."

But Daniel couldn't move. His eyes were transfixed on the light, drawn to it in a way that made his chest tighten. The pendant around his neck was vibrating now, humming with the same energy that radiated from the glowing light.

"It's not letting us leave," Daniel whispered, more to himself than to the others.

The door to freedom was right there, just beyond the light. But the energy in the room felt like an impenetrable wall, blocking their path. And Daniel knew, deep down, that this wasn't the Order's doing. This was something older, something far more powerful.

"It's a trap," Marcus said, panic edging into his voice.

"No," Daniel said, shaking his head. "It's not a trap. It's a test."

He could feel it now, the weight of the Ascendant's power pressing down on him, challenging him. This was part of the ritual, part of the bond that had been forged the moment he touched the pendant. He had to prove himself—to the power, to the ancestors, to the relic itself.

And if he failed...

"There's no way out unless I complete this," Daniel said, his voice steady despite the fear that churned in his gut. "Stay back."

"What are you going to do?" Evelyn asked, her eyes wide with concern.

"I don't know," Daniel admitted. "But I have to do it."

He stepped forward, toward the light, his hand still clutching the pendant. The energy in the room seemed to pulse in time with his heartbeat, growing stronger with each step he took. When he was close enough to feel the warmth of the light on his skin, he stopped. The pendant hummed in his hand, and Daniel knew what he had to do. He closed his eyes and let go.

Chapter 17: Shadows of Legacy

For a moment, there was nothing but silence. Daniel stood in the cavern, the blinding light surrounding him, its warmth wrapping around his body like a cocoon. His heart raced, the beat pounding in his ears, yet there was an eerie calm to the air—as if the entire world had been suspended in time. His fingers tingled from where he had released the pendant, the sensation spreading through his body like an electric current. He didn't move. He didn't dare breathe. Every fiber of his being was focused on the energy that now coursed through the chamber. This was it—his test, his moment of reckoning. And failure wasn't an option. The pendant floated before him, suspended in midair, the glow from the light intensifying around it. It rotated slowly, the intricate carvings catching the faintest glimmer of the flickering light. Daniel could feel the pull of the Ascendant deep within his bones, urging him forward, urging him to connect with the power that now hummed in the air. But the moment his hand twitched, intending to reach for it, a voice—a deep, resonant voice—filled the cavern. It echoed off the stone walls, ancient and commanding, like the voice of someone who had lived a thousand lives.

"You are not ready."

Daniel's breath caught in his throat, his heart pounding harder now. He couldn't see the source of the voice, but it was there, all around him, pressing against his mind.

"What do you mean?" he called out, his voice trembling despite himself. "I've made it this far. I've taken the pendant."

The voice did not answer right away. Instead, the light in the chamber dimmed, casting long shadows across the walls. The pendant remained suspended, but its glow was weaker now, almost as if it, too, was waiting for something.

"Power alone does not make one worthy." The voice was closer now, almost whispering in Daniel's ear. "It is the strength of your heart, the purity of your will."

Daniel swallowed hard, his palms slick with sweat. His chest tightened as he processed the words. He had known from the beginning that this wasn't going to be easy, but now, standing here, he felt the weight of every decision he had made since stepping foot on this path.

"I can do this," Daniel whispered, more to himself than to the voice. "I have to."

"Are you willing to face the truth?" the voice asked, its tone hardening. "Are you ready to face the sins of your bloodline, to accept what was done in your name?"

Daniel blinked, confusion washing over him. "What are you talking about?"

Suddenly, the chamber shifted. The stone walls flickered like a mirage, and in an instant, Daniel was no longer in the cavern. The cold, damp air was replaced by the heat of a blazing sun, and the echo of dripping water was drowned out by the deafening roar of battle. He was standing in the middle of a battlefield. Bodies littered the ground around him—men, women, and children alike, their blood soaking into the scorched earth. The air was thick with the smell of death, and the sky above was darkened by smoke. In the distance, a great city burned, its towers collapsing in on themselves as flames consumed everything in their path. Daniel turned, his eyes wide with horror. This wasn't a vision. This was real. He could feel the heat of the fire on his skin, could smell the coppery tang of blood in the air. His heart raced, panic rising in his chest.

"What is this?" he shouted. "Where am I?"

"This is the legacy of the Ascendant," the voice replied, its tone heavy with sorrow. "This is the price of power."

Daniel's stomach churned as he watched the scene unfold around him. Soldiers clad in the armor of the Ascendant House stormed through the battlefield, their swords flashing in the dim light as they cut down anyone who stood in their way. The screams of the dying echoed in his ears, each one more haunting than the last.

"Your ancestors sought power at any cost," the voice continued. "They destroyed entire kingdoms, slaughtered innocent people, all in the name of the Ascendant. This is the bloodline you were born into, the legacy you now carry."

"No," Daniel breathed, shaking his head in disbelief. "That's not true. The Ascendant was supposed to protect people. They were guardians."

"They were conquerors." The voice was merciless now, the weight of its judgment pressing down on Daniel like a physical force. "Your family betrayed the very people they were meant to protect. They used the power of the relics to subjugate entire nations. This is what you inherit, Daniel. This is the truth of the Ascendant."

Daniel stumbled backward, his mind reeling. His entire life, he had been taught that the Ascendant were noble, that his bloodline had been entrusted with great power to protect the world from chaos. But now, standing in the middle of this nightmare, he saw the truth for what it really was. His ancestors had been monsters. Tears stung his eyes as he watched a soldier—a man who bore the same crest as the pendant—cut down a helpless woman, her cries silenced in an instant. This was what his family had done. This was the power they had wielded. And now that same power was in his hands.

"Do you still wish to wield the power of the Ascendant?" the voice asked, its tone quieter now, almost gentle. "Do you wish to continue this legacy?"

Daniel's chest tightened, his breath coming in ragged gasps. The pendant hung heavy around his neck, its weight more suffocating than ever before. He could feel the power coursing through it, but now it felt tainted, corrupted by the sins of his ancestors.

He didn't want this. He didn't want to be like them.

"I'm not like them," Daniel whispered, clenching his fists. "I won't be."

"The power of the Ascendant will consume you, just as it consumed them," the voice warned. "Unless you are strong enough to resist it."

Daniel took a deep breath, forcing himself to steady his racing heart. The images of the battlefield flickered around him, the heat and noise fading into the background as he focused on the pendant. His fingers closed around it, the metal cool against his skin.

"I won't let it control me," he said, his voice stronger now. "I'll use it to make things right. To fix what my ancestors did."

The voice was silent for a moment, as if considering his words.

"Then prove it."

The world shifted again, and Daniel was back in the cavern, the light surrounding him once more. But this time, it was different. The warmth of the light was no longer comforting—it was scorching, burning him from the inside out. The pendant in his hand pulsed with energy, more powerful than before, as if testing his resolve. Daniel gritted his teeth, his body shaking from the intensity of the power that surged through him. He could feel it pulling at him, trying to consume him, just as the voice had warned. The weight of his ancestors' sins pressed down on him, threatening to crush him under its burden. But he refused to let it. With a fierce cry, Daniel closed his eyes and focused on the pendant, channeling all of his will into controlling the power. He could feel it fighting against him, like a raging storm, but he held firm. He wasn't going to let the past define him. He wasn't going to be like his ancestors. Slowly, the heat began to subside, the light dimming as Daniel regained control. His body trembled with exhaustion, but he stood tall, his grip on the pendant unyielding. When the light finally faded, Daniel opened his eyes. The cavern was quiet once more. The voice was gone, and the pendant hung loosely from his neck, no longer pulsing with energy. He had done it. He had passed the test. Evelyn and Marcus stared at him in stunned silence, their faces pale with shock.

"Daniel?" Evelyn whispered, her voice barely audible.

"I'm still here," Daniel said, his voice hoarse but steady. He took a deep breath, his chest heaving. "I'm still me."

For now.

Chapter 18: Fractured Paths

The weight of silence pressed down on the trio as they stood in the dimly lit cavern. Daniel felt the air shift, as if the very earth beneath them was holding its breath. His mind raced, replaying the events that had just unfolded—the battle within himself, the revelation of his ancestors' atrocities. He clenched his fists, feeling the cold metal of the pendant brush against his knuckles. It was no longer a symbol of power. It was a burden. Evelyn moved first, stepping toward Daniel cautiously, as though afraid of what he might say or do.

"You... you passed, didn't you?" Her voice was soft, but there was a tremor behind it, a ripple of fear she couldn't quite hide.

Daniel didn't answer immediately. His gaze was fixed on the pendant, its faint glow barely perceptible now. "I don't know," he replied, his voice low. "I don't know what passing really means anymore."

Marcus, leaning heavily against the cavern wall, grimaced in pain but forced himself to speak. "It means you're still here. You're still you. And whatever that voice was, you didn't let it break you."

"I almost did," Daniel muttered. He shook his head, the memories of the vision still vivid. The battlefield, the destruction, the screams of the innocent... it was all too real. His ancestors had been conquerors, not protectors. He had seen it with his own eyes. He felt a deep, gnawing anger, not just toward the Order, but toward the very bloodline he came from.

Evelyn looked at him with concern. "What did it show you?"

Daniel met her eyes. "The truth," he said bitterly. "Everything we've been told about the Ascendant? The tales of heroism, of protecting the people? It's all a lie. My ancestors... they were murderers. They destroyed entire kingdoms, wiped out families, all for power."

The cavern fell silent again. The revelation hung in the air like a thick fog, impossible to escape.

"We need to keep moving," Marcus said, breaking the tension. "If the Order isn't already on our trail, they will be soon. And we don't want to be here when they catch up."

Daniel nodded, pushing the thoughts of his bloodline aside, at least for now. "The passage leads out through the forest," he said, his voice firmer. "Once we're clear of the estate, we can regroup and figure out our next move."

Evelyn hesitated, glancing at Marcus. "Are you sure you can make it?"

Marcus gave a strained chuckle. "I've survived worse. Let's just get the hell out of here."

The trio made their way toward the door at the end of the cavern. The wooden structure was ancient, barely hanging on its hinges, and the air that seeped through the cracks was cool and fresh, a stark contrast to the oppressive heat of the chamber they were leaving behind. Daniel reached for the handle, the rusted metal cold against his palm, and pushed. The door groaned, the wood splintering slightly as it swung open to reveal a narrow passageway lined with damp stone. A faint light flickered at the far end, barely visible but enough to give them hope that freedom was near. They moved cautiously, the weight of the pendant a constant reminder of what they had just endured. Each step Daniel took felt heavier than the last, as if the truth of his heritage was physically weighing him down. His thoughts churned, trying to reconcile the stories he had been told his whole life with the brutal reality he had witnessed. As they neared the exit, the sound of rustling leaves and the distant call of birds reached their ears. It was a welcome relief after the suffocating stillness of the underground chamber. The passage opened up into a dense forest, the trees towering above them like ancient sentinels, their branches swaying gently in the breeze.

"We're close," Daniel said, his eyes scanning the treeline. "The Order won't be far behind. We need to keep moving."

But before they could take another step, a voice—sharp and familiar—rang out from behind them.

"Not so fast."

Daniel spun around, his heart sinking as he saw them. Standing at the mouth of the passage, blocking their escape, were two figures clad in dark robes—the unmistakable insignia of the Order gleaming on their chests. Their faces were obscured by hoods, but the cold, calculating glint in their eyes was all too familiar.

One of them stepped forward, lowering their hood to reveal a woman with sharp features and eyes that gleamed with dangerous intent. "Did you really think you could escape us, Daniel? You've become too valuable to let go."

Evelyn reached for her dagger, but Daniel held out his arm, stopping her. His pulse quickened, but he forced himself to remain calm. "I'm not going with you," he said, his voice steady. "And you're not getting the Ascendant."

The woman's lips curled into a cruel smile. "Oh, I don't think you have much of a choice. You've bonded with the pendant now. That makes you a threat—and a target."

Marcus shifted behind Daniel, his hand gripping his side where his wound was still bleeding. "We don't have time for this, Daniel. We need to—"

Before he could finish, the second figure raised a hand, and the air around them seemed to ripple with power. A shockwave surged through the clearing, knocking Marcus and Evelyn off their feet. Daniel barely managed to brace himself, stumbling backward but staying upright.

"Enough of this," the woman snapped, her voice like ice. "Hand over the pendant, or we'll take it by force."

Daniel's hand instinctively went to the pendant around his neck, his fingers curling around the cool metal. The energy within it pulsed faintly, as though responding to the threat before him. He could feel the power—vast, overwhelming, and dangerous—waiting just beneath the surface. He could use it. He could end this right now. But something held him back. The vision of the battlefield flashed in his mind once more, the screams of the innocent ringing in his ears. He had seen what the power of the Ascendant could do. He had seen the destruction it could unleash. If he wasn't careful, he could become just like his ancestors—drunk on power, blind to the consequences.

"I won't use it," Daniel muttered under his breath, more to himself than to anyone else.

The woman's eyes narrowed. "What was that?"

Daniel straightened, his grip on the pendant tightening. "I said I won't use it. I'm not like you. I won't let the Ascendant's power control me."

The woman's smile faded, replaced by a look of cold fury. "Then you're a fool."

With a swift motion, she raised her hand, and the ground beneath them began to tremble. The trees swayed violently, the wind howling through the clearing as the power of the Order surged through the air. Daniel's heart raced. He could feel the pendant vibrating against his chest, the power inside it reacting to the energy around him. He had a choice—use the Ascendant's power to fight back or risk being overpowered. But before he could make his decision, a new voice—familiar and commanding—rang out from the shadows.

"Leave him."

All eyes turned to the treeline, where a lone figure stepped forward, their features obscured by the dim light of the forest. But Daniel recognized the voice instantly. It was his uncle, Richard.

Chapter 19: The Unseen Hand

Richard's presence was both a relief and a mystery. His calm, unwavering posture contrasted sharply with the chaos swirling in Daniel's mind. Standing at the edge of the clearing, cloaked in shadow, Richard seemed unaffected by the tension gripping the air. His eyes, cold and calculating, swept over the Order's agents as if assessing their every move.

The woman from the Order, however, was not easily rattled. She crossed her arms, her stance defiant. "Richard," she said, her voice laced with venom. "You shouldn't be here. You're supposed to be dead."

Richard let out a low chuckle, stepping forward with the grace of a predator. "Dead? Come now, Victoria. You should know better than to believe the rumors the Order spreads. You've always been smarter than that."

Victoria's eyes narrowed. "You're a traitor."

Richard's smile didn't falter. "A traitor? Or a man who saw the truth behind the lies?" His gaze shifted to Daniel, lingering for a moment, before returning to the Order agents. "I won't let you take him. The Ascendant's power isn't yours to control anymore."

The tension in the air thickened, the wind howling through the trees as if in response to the power that now vibrated between the opposing forces. Daniel's pulse quickened as he glanced between his uncle and the Order agents, the weight of the pendant growing heavier around his neck.

Victoria seemed to hesitate for the briefest moment, her jaw clenched as though considering her options. Then her eyes darkened, and a wicked smile tugged at the corners of her mouth. "You always were a stubborn fool, Richard. But this time, you won't walk away."

With a sharp motion of her hand, the air shimmered, and suddenly, the second agent lunged forward. Daniel barely had time to react. He saw the flash of movement, the glint of a blade in the fading light, and instinctively raised his hand. The pendant flared to life, a surge of raw energy pulsing through him as the air around him crackled with power. Before the blade could reach him, a force field erupted between Daniel and the agent, sending the man flying backward. The impact was brutal, his body slamming into a nearby tree with a sickening thud. Daniel's heart pounded in his chest as he stared at his hands, still trembling from the sheer force of the power he had unleashed. He hadn't meant to use it. But now that he had, the surge of power coursing through him was intoxicating, almost overwhelming.

"Daniel, no!" Richard's voice cut through the haze of energy, sharp and commanding. His eyes locked onto Daniel, a warning flashing in their depths. "Don't give in to it. The power will consume you if you let it."

Daniel gritted his teeth, forcing himself to release the pendant. The energy around him flickered and dissipated, leaving him breathless and shaken. He didn't want this power, but it seemed to have a will of its own, reacting to his emotions, feeding on his fear.

Victoria's lips twisted into a sneer as she straightened, brushing the dust from her robes. "You can't protect him forever, Richard. The boy is already in too deep. The Ascendant's power is too strong—he'll lose himself to it, just like all the others."

Richard took a step forward, his gaze cold and unyielding. "He won't. I'll make sure of it."

The tension between them crackled like a live wire, both sides poised to strike. Daniel felt his muscles coil, ready for whatever came next, but before another blow could be struck, a distant sound broke through the stillness. Hoofbeats. Dozens of them. The Order agents stiffened, their heads snapping toward the forest's edge. Through the thick canopy of trees, the faint flicker of torches appeared, growing brighter and more numerous by the second. Reinforcements were coming.

"We're out of time," Richard muttered under his breath. "We need to go. Now."

Victoria's eyes gleamed with satisfaction. "You'll never escape the Order, Richard. Not this time."

Richard's jaw tightened, his fists clenching at his sides. "Watch me."

Without another word, Richard spun on his heel and grabbed Daniel by the arm, pulling him away from the clearing and deeper into the forest. Evelyn and Marcus followed closely, their footsteps quick and silent as they disappeared into the shadows. The sound of the approaching riders grew louder, the ground beneath their feet vibrating with the force of the coming storm. They ran in silence, the forest around them thick and suffocating. Daniel's mind raced, his thoughts a whirlwind of confusion and fear. His uncle had been alive this entire time, hiding in the shadows, watching as the Order hunted them. But why now? Why had Richard revealed himself at this moment? And what did he know about the Ascendant's power that he wasn't telling them? After what felt like an eternity of running, Richard finally slowed, guiding them toward a small, hidden clearing. The trees here were denser, their branches creating a thick canopy that blocked out most of the light. They were safe for the moment.

Richard released Daniel's arm and turned to face him, his expression hard but unreadable. "We don't have much time, so listen carefully," he said, his voice low and urgent. "The Order won't stop until they have the pendant. They'll hunt you to the ends of the earth if they have to. But you can't let them take it. Do you understand?"

Daniel nodded, still trying to catch his breath. "But why? Why is the pendant so important?"

Richard's gaze flickered to the pendant around Daniel's neck, his expression darkening. "The pendant is the key to unlocking the full power of the Ascendant. Whoever controls it controls the fate of the world."

Evelyn stepped forward, her brow furrowed in confusion. "But the Order already has other relics. Why is this one so special?"

"Because this pendant doesn't just contain power—it contains knowledge. The knowledge of every Ascendant who ever lived. The Order wants that knowledge, but they won't use it for good. They'll twist it, corrupt it, just like they did in the past."

Daniel felt a chill run down his spine. The weight of the pendant around his neck seemed to grow heavier with every word his uncle spoke.

"So what do we do now?" Marcus asked, his voice strained from pain. "We can't keep running forever."

Richard's expression hardened. "No, we can't. But there's a place—a sanctuary. It's hidden deep in the mountains, a place where the Order can't reach us. If we can make it there, we'll have time to regroup, to figure out how to destroy the pendant before the Order gets their hands on it."

"Destroy it?" Daniel repeated, his heart skipping a beat. "But you said—"

"I know what I said," Richard interrupted, his tone sharp. "But the power of the Ascendant is too dangerous. If we don't destroy it, the world will suffer for it. We don't have a choice."

Daniel's mind reeled. Everything he had been told about the Ascendant, about his bloodline, was crumbling before him. He had spent his life believing he was destined for greatness, that the power of the Ascendant would bring balance and protection to the world. But now, all he saw was the destruction it had caused—the lives it had ruined.

"I don't know if I can do this," Daniel whispered, his voice barely audible.

Richard placed a firm hand on his shoulder, his eyes softening for the first time since he had appeared. "You don't have to do it alone, Daniel. We're in this together. But you have to trust me."

Daniel looked into his uncle's eyes, searching for some sign of reassurance, some hint that this nightmare would soon end. But all he saw was the weight of the choices they had yet to make. In the distance, the sound of hoofbeats grew closer.

Chapter 20: The Chase Begins

The thundering of hooves became a low, constant rumble in the distance, a pulse of danger growing closer with every passing second. Daniel's heart pounded in his chest as his mind raced, trying to process the whirlwind of revelations that had just been thrown at him. His uncle was alive. The Order was closing in. And the pendant around his neck, the very thing he had been raised to believe was a symbol of salvation, had now become a ticking time bomb.

"How far is this sanctuary?" Evelyn asked, her voice cutting through the tense silence.

Richard scanned the trees, his jaw tight. "It's not close. At least two days' journey through the mountains, maybe more if we're careful."

"Two days?" Marcus groaned, leaning heavily against a tree. He wiped a hand across his brow, which was damp with sweat, his face pale from his injuries. "I don't think I can make it that long."

"You have to," Richard said bluntly. "The Order won't stop until they have that pendant, and if they catch us, they won't show mercy."

"We've been running for months," Daniel said, his voice hardening as he looked at his uncle. "You've been watching us this whole time, haven't you? Why didn't you step in sooner? Why now?"

Richard met his gaze, the shadows of the forest deepening the lines on his face. "Because I needed to be sure. I had to know if you were ready—if you could handle the truth."

Daniel clenched his fists. "And what if I wasn't? What if the Order had killed us before you decided to show up?"

His uncle's expression softened slightly, but there was a glimmer of something unreadable in his eyes. "I was never far. I would've intervened before it got to that point."

Evelyn stepped forward, her eyes flashing with frustration. "We don't have time for this. The Order is almost here, and we need to get moving. Whatever issues you two have, deal with them later."

Daniel opened his mouth to argue but stopped himself. She was right. This wasn't the time to hash out family betrayals or hidden agendas. They needed to survive first.

"Fine," Daniel said, his voice tight. "But this conversation isn't over."

Richard nodded, his expression unreadable. "Understood. But for now, we need to move quickly and quietly. The Order has scouts combing the forest—they'll surround us if we're not careful."

Without waiting for another word, Richard turned and led them deeper into the forest. The dense canopy overhead filtered the fading daylight into dim patches of gold and green, casting long shadows across the forest floor. Every branch that snapped underfoot, every rustle of leaves in the wind felt like a signal to their enemies. Daniel's senses were heightened, his body thrumming with the same nervous energy that had flooded him back in the cavern. He couldn't shake the feeling that they were being watched, hunted.

"Stay close," Richard called over his shoulder. "We're heading toward the river. If we can reach it before nightfall, we can use the current to mask our trail."

They moved quickly, slipping between the trees like shadows. The forest seemed to stretch endlessly in every direction, the ancient trunks towering above them, their roots twisting beneath the earth like veins. Every now and then, Daniel would catch a flicker of movement from the corner of his eye—a bird darting between the branches, or perhaps something else. As the hours passed, the sound of the hoofbeats faded, replaced by the steady hum of the forest at dusk. But the tension never left Daniel's body. He kept his eyes on his uncle, watching the way Richard moved with purpose and certainty, as if he knew these woods like the back of his hand.

"I don't trust him," Marcus muttered under his breath as he walked beside Daniel, his face pale and lined with pain.

Daniel glanced at him, frowning. "He's my uncle. He saved us."

"Maybe," Marcus said, his voice low. "But he's been hiding for months, watching us from the shadows. He didn't come out of nowhere. He has his own agenda."

Evelyn, overhearing their conversation, shot Marcus a sharp look. "Now isn't the time for suspicion. We need to stay together."

"I'm just saying," Marcus added, his voice trailing off as he winced from the pain in his side. "People don't just disappear unless they're hiding something."

Daniel's stomach twisted. Marcus wasn't wrong. His uncle had been hiding something—something important. And the more they ran, the more Daniel's mind buzzed with unanswered questions. But for now, survival came first. They moved in silence for what felt like hours, the sun dipping lower and lower in the sky until the world was bathed in twilight. The forest grew darker, the sounds of insects and distant animals filling the air as the temperature began to drop. Daniel could hear the faint rush of water in the distance, a sign that they were getting close to the river Richard had mentioned.

"We're almost there," Richard said, his voice quiet but steady. "Once we reach the river, we'll find a spot to cross and set up camp on the other side. The Order won't expect us to move after nightfall."

Evelyn nodded. "Good. I could use a few hours of rest."

But just as the promise of safety began to settle in Daniel's mind, a sharp crack echoed through the trees—like the snap of a branch underfoot. The group froze. Daniel's heart skipped a beat as his eyes darted toward the source of the noise. Richard's hand shot up, signaling them to stay still. His eyes scanned the surrounding trees, his body tense, ready for action. For a moment, there was nothing—just the rustle of leaves in the wind. But then, out of the darkness, came a low growl, deep and guttural. It was followed by the unmistakable sound of movement—something large, moving through the underbrush.

Daniel's blood turned cold.

"What was that?" Marcus whispered, his voice barely audible.

Richard didn't respond. His eyes narrowed as he pulled a dagger from his belt, the blade gleaming faintly in the fading light. He motioned for the others to stay behind him, his posture alert, every muscle coiled for action. The growling grew louder, and from the shadows emerged a figure—at first just a silhouette, hulking and misshapen. But as it stepped into the dim light filtering through the trees, Daniel's heart leapt into his throat. It wasn't human. The creature was massive, standing on two legs like a man, but its skin was mottled and gray, covered in thick, matted fur. Its face was elongated, with sharp, pointed teeth glistening in the dim light, and its eyes—deep, glowing red—locked onto them with an unnatural intelligence. Clawed hands flexed at its sides, ready to tear through anything in its path. A cold chill ran down Daniel's spine. He had heard stories of creatures like this—beasts summoned by dark magic, twisted and corrupted by those who wielded forbidden power. But he had never seen one up close.

"Wraithhound," Richard muttered under his breath, his voice tense. "Stay back."

Before anyone could move, the creature let out a deafening roar, its powerful legs launching it forward with terrifying speed. Daniel's instincts kicked in. He grabbed Evelyn by the arm and pulled her back just as the beast lunged, its claws raking through the air where she had been standing moments before. Marcus staggered backward, his face pale with shock as he raised his sword, but Richard was faster. In a blur of motion, Richard darted forward, his dagger flashing as he slashed at the creature's flank. The beast howled in pain, stumbling to the side, but it quickly recovered, its glowing red eyes locking onto Richard with deadly intent.

"Get to the river!" Richard shouted over his shoulder. "Now!"

Daniel didn't need to be told twice. He grabbed Evelyn's hand and bolted toward the sound of rushing water, his heart pounding in his chest. Marcus followed close behind, limping as he struggled to keep up, but the adrenaline surging through his body kept him moving. The roar of the river grew louder, the sound of rushing water filling Daniel's ears as they burst through the trees and onto the riverbank. The current was strong, the water cold and churning as it rushed over rocks and fallen branches.

"We need to cross," Daniel said, his voice breathless. "It'll slow the beast down."

Evelyn glanced at the river, her eyes wide with fear. "But Marcus—"

"I can make it," Marcus said through gritted teeth, hobbling forward. "Go."

Without another word, Daniel waded into the river, the icy water biting at his legs as the current pushed against him. He kept his grip on Evelyn's hand, pulling her forward as they fought their way across, the water rising to their waists as they moved deeper into the rushing stream. Behind them, the growls and roars of the wraithhound grew louder, mixed with the sounds of Richard's voice shouting commands. But then—just as Daniel and Evelyn reached the middle of the river—there was a sharp, piercing scream. Daniel froze, his blood turning to ice as he whipped around to see Marcus, standing at the edge of the riverbank, his eyes wide with terror. The beast had broken through. The scream tore through the night, freezing Daniel in place as he watched the beast barrel toward Marcus. Time seemed to slow, the roar of the river a dull roar in the background as the world narrowed to the terrifying scene on the bank. Marcus raised his sword in desperation, but the wraithhound was too fast, too strong. It knocked him off his feet, sending him crashing into the ground. The air left his lungs in a pained gasp as the beast loomed over him, its claws poised for the killing blow.

"Marcus!" Evelyn screamed, but she was powerless, her hand still gripped tightly in Daniel's as they stood in the middle of the river.

Without thinking, Daniel reached for the pendant. He didn't have time to be afraid, didn't have time to second-guess himself. All that mattered was stopping the creature before it killed Marcus—before it killed all of them. The moment his fingers closed around the pendant, a surge of power pulsed through him, stronger than anything he had felt before. It was wild and untamed, like a storm raging inside him, but he didn't fight it this time. He let the power flow through him, his mind clear and focused. With a shout, Daniel thrust his free hand toward the beast. A blinding flash of light erupted from his palm, striking the creature square in the chest. The wraithhound howled in pain, stumbling backward as the light engulfed it. Its body convulsed, writhing as the magic tore through it, and then—with one final, ear-piercing scream—it disintegrated into a cloud of ash. The clearing fell into a stunned silence, the only sound the rush of the river and the distant wind. Daniel stood frozen, his heart racing, his breath coming in ragged gasps. The power still hummed in his veins, but it had receded, no longer threatening to overwhelm him. He had done it.

"Marcus!" Evelyn broke free of Daniel's grip and rushed to the riverbank, dropping to her knees beside Marcus. He was alive, but barely. Blood trickled from a deep gash on his leg, his face pale and drenched in sweat.

Richard appeared from the shadows, his face grim as he knelt beside Marcus, quickly assessing the wound. "It's bad," he muttered, tearing a strip of cloth from his cloak to bandage the injury. "We need to stop the bleeding."

Evelyn looked up, her eyes wide and pleading. "Can you help him?"

Richard's jaw tightened as he worked. "I'll do what I can, but he needs a healer. We can't stay here."

Daniel stared at his uncle, the reality of what had just happened slowly sinking in. The beast was gone. The Order was still chasing them. And now Marcus was gravely injured. The sanctuary Richard had mentioned felt farther away than ever.

"What now?" Daniel asked, his voice hoarse.

Richard glanced up, meeting his eyes. "We keep moving. The Order won't stop just because the wraithhound is dead. They'll be here soon, and they'll bring more with them."

Daniel's heart sank. He had hoped, for a brief moment, that destroying the beast might have given them some reprieve. But the fight was far from over.

"We have to cross the river," Richard continued, standing and pulling Marcus to his feet. "The current will help mask our trail."

Evelyn and Daniel exchanged a look, both of them exhausted, but there was no other option. They couldn't stay here. They couldn't stop. Together, they helped Marcus across the river, the cold water biting at their legs as they struggled against the current. Richard led the way, his eyes constantly scanning the trees, alert for any sign of danger. By the time they reached the other side, night had fully fallen, casting the forest in deep shadows.

"We need to find shelter," Richard said once they were safely across. "Somewhere to hide until Marcus can walk on his own."

Daniel nodded, though every part of him ached with fatigue. They had been running for what felt like forever, and the weight of the pendant around his neck seemed to grow heavier with every step. As they moved deeper into the forest, Daniel's mind churned with unanswered questions. What had the pendant truly done to him? Was he now bound to its power forever? And how much longer could they keep running before the Order finally caught up to them? He glanced at Richard, who was walking ahead, his face a mask of steely determination. His uncle knew more than he was letting on—Daniel was sure of it. But right now, the only thing that mattered was surviving. Hours passed in silence as they trudged through the dense forest. Marcus's condition worsened, his steps faltering more and more as he leaned heavily on Evelyn and Daniel for support. Every so often, Richard would glance back at them, but he said nothing, his focus entirely on finding a place to rest. Finally, just as dawn began to break over the horizon, they came upon a small cave nestled in the side of a hill. It was barely large enough for the four of them, but it offered shelter from the elements and, more importantly, a place to hide.

"This will have to do," Richard said as he helped Marcus into the cave and gently lowered him to the ground. "We'll rest here for a few hours, then continue at first light."

Daniel sank down beside Marcus, exhaustion washing over him. His body ached, his mind numb from everything that had happened. Evelyn sat beside him, her head resting against the cave wall as her eyes fluttered shut. For the first time in what felt like days, the forest was quiet. No hoofbeats, no growls, no echoes of pursuit. Just the faint rustle of leaves in the breeze and the soft, steady rhythm of the river in the distance. As Daniel sat there, his thoughts drifted back to the pendant around his neck. It pulsed faintly against his skin, a constant reminder of the power it held—and the danger it posed. He had to destroy it. But how? Richard's words echoed in his mind: The pendant contains knowledge. The knowledge of every Ascendant who ever lived. Could that knowledge be the key to its destruction? Or would it only lead him deeper into the very darkness they were trying to escape? Daniel's eyes drifted closed, his mind heavy with questions and doubts. But one thing was certain: the fight wasn't over. Not yet. As sleep finally claimed him, Daniel's last thought was of the journey ahead—the sanctuary, the Order, and the secret that lay buried within the pendant. Whatever happened next, he would be ready.

About the Author

I have been wanting to write books for a while but never knew how. When writing a book, I always go with something random and don't always know what I want to write about. Sometimes there are a lot of different reasons for this, but for me personally, I just think of something random and go with it. There are times when I will use an AI to help me, but I was just messing around. I love how this book turned out and I hope you enjoy it.

Milton Keynes UK
Ingram Content Group UK Ltd.
UKHW020406021124
450424UK00014B/1451